Dr. Daisy H. Digg

Moving the Mountain

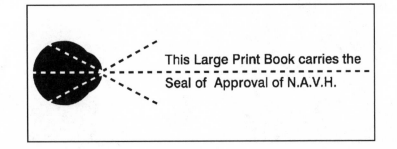

This Large Print Book carries the
Seal of Approval of N.A.V.H.

KENTUCKY BRIDES, BOOK 3

Moving the Mountain

ROMANCE COMPLICATES A
SIMPLE WAY OF HISTORIC LIFE

Yvonne Lehman

THORNDIKE PRESS
A part of Gale, Cengage Learning

Detroit • New York • San Francisco • New Haven, Conn • Waterville, Maine • London

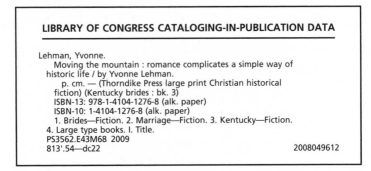

LIBRARY OF CONGRESS CATALOGING-IN-PUBLICATION DATA

Lehman, Yvonne.
  Moving the mountain : romance complicates a simple way of historic life / by Yvonne Lehman.
    p. cm. — (Thorndike Press large print Christian historical fiction) (Kentucky brides : bk. 3)
  ISBN-13: 978-1-4104-1276-8 (alk. paper)
  ISBN-10: 1-4104-1276-8 (alk. paper)
  1. Brides—Fiction. 2. Marriage—Fiction. 3. Kentucky—Fiction.
  4. Large type books. I. Title.
  PS3562.E43M68 2009
  813'.54—dc22   2008049612

Published in 2009 by arrangement with Barbour Publishing, Inc.

Printed in the United States of America
1 2 3 4 5 6 7 13 12 11 10 09

Dedication

A special thanks to Jeanette Cloud for her expertise on Harlan County, Kentucky, and my writers' group (Ann, Debbie, Lisa, Lori, and Michelle) for their helpful comments.

ONE

"Life's not hard," Jonas McLean said to his horse. "It's impossible."

Unable to concentrate on the May 24, 1912, *Weekly Enterprise* he'd just purchased at the Poplar Grove Depot, he tossed it into the back of the wagon.

Thoughts of Molly Pierpont clouded his mind. She would arrive any moment, and he could do nothing to prevent it.

He hadn't known how to deal with Sarah's dying wish. His wife had made him promise to ask her sister, Molly, to help take care of Dawn and Caleb if anything happened to her.

Sarah must have had a premonition because she died in childbirth nine months ago, along with their baby. Molly had offered to stay after the funeral, but Jonas insisted he could take care of his own daughter and son just fine. After all, Dawn had just turned nine and could handle two-year-old Caleb while Jonas plowed his fields, planted his crops, and cared for his farm animals.

Three months ago, Jonas received a telegram from Molly. Her husband, Percival Pierpont, had met with an untimely death. By the time he retrieved the telegram from town, the funeral would have been over. He'd telegrammed his condolences.

Although he and Percival hadn't related well on the one occasion he'd visited along with Molly, Jonas was sorry to hear of anyone's untimely death. But he hadn't had to worry about Molly showing up to help where she wasn't needed.

During the winter months and spring rains, he was pretty much confined to the cabin with the children. A neighbor came by to take Dawn to school since Jonas took a leave of absence from teaching history at Pine Hollow and Coalville schools. He didn't see how he could return until Caleb reached school age. Those were hard months without Sarah, but he felt with time, they'd adjust.

They would have if Dawn hadn't attempted to roll an iron pot up a hill. She lost her grip, slid, tried to catch it, and the weight of it broke a bone near her elbow. The doctor said the bone having protruded through the skin put her at risk for infection.

Neighbors would help if he asked, but they had their own lives to live. Also, this was planting season. Trying to be positive, Jonas reminded himself that at least school was out for the summer. But for the past week, Dawn was either in pain or so drowsy from the laudanum she could do nothing but lie around.

Reluctantly, Jonas had made a visit to the impressive house in the city to express his sympathy and ask Molly to help out for a couple of weeks, just until he could get additional planting done and look for someone to handle Caleb.

He didn't expect that a twenty-four-year-old city woman like Molly could adjust to life back in the cove of Kentucky's Appalachian Mountains — not even for a couple of weeks. But Sarah had made him promise to ask.

When Sarah and the baby died, he'd thought things couldn't get worse. But they had.

Dawn had enough trouble handling Caleb when he was only two. After he turned three, he gained experience and delighted in getting into everything. Jonas had faith in God, but not in having to take in a city woman who knew nothing of hunting for supper in the forest, fishing from the creeks, or the rearing of children.

At least Molly had two good arms. He knew what his children needed most was someone to help them stop crying themselves to sleep every night. He had his doubts about that since he didn't expect anyone or anything to ease the ache of loss he felt deep within his heart.

He knew nothing about how to treat a city woman. Not one who wore silly hats, frilly clothes, and carried a parasol.

If only Sarah hadn't made him promise to ask . . .

His anxiety grew when the whistle blew and the train came protesting, chugging and huffing around the mountain with black smoke curling from its stack. Jonas took a deep breath, feeling like a weight was on his chest. He wouldn't be surprised to see a puff of black smoke come out of his lungs.

Molly attempted to look as morose as the black mourning clothes she wore. Many of her acquaintances would be mortified to think she'd dress otherwise for less than a year. However, upon glimpsing her reflection in the train window, she warned herself to get that happy expression off her face.

She must indeed be an ingrate, being so eager to leave behind the kind of life for which she'd often been told she should be grateful. Her sights were set on the challenge ahead.

No one ever understood her — except Sarah. And she hadn't been allowed to see her until the past few years, then only once or twice a year. That thought wiped the smile from her lips. She should wear black for Sarah, if not for her deceased husband.

She'd been told through the years, "Look on the bright side. Count your blessings."

Molly decided to do that now. Her excitement heightened as did the scenery. She'd watched the change from valleys of bluegrass to high hills and then the craggy mountain peaks of Harlan County.

She thought of the times when she'd stepped from the train at Poplar Grove Depot that was surrounded by Kentucky's forested mountains. Sarah would come running to give Molly the kind of hug and welcome she longed for.

The last time she came was nine months ago for Sarah's funeral. Aunt Mae accompanied her, without Percy who said he couldn't get away from business. A few of Jonas's relatives had arrived on the same

11

train. They made a somber appearance, all dressed in black, riding up the mountain in rented black carriages.

This time, Molly told herself not to think of Sarah's absence, but of the presence of Jonas and his children.

The train pulled around the last bend. The whistle blew as if in celebration. Molly thought she couldn't get any happier, but when the train's rhythmic movement slowed until it stopped at the depot, she felt her heart might burst with anticipation.

As soon as she stepped from the train and her pointed-toe shoes touched the hard-packed earth, a pine-scented wind whipped her long skirt to the side, and she touched her hat to keep it from blowing away.

She laughed, gripping her gift-bearing bag.

Her laughter caught in her throat when she saw no children. Jonas, looking like the life had gone out of him, ambled toward her. His broad shoulders slumped, as they had at Sarah's funeral.

A stab of regret washed over her. For a moment she allowed her own loss to linger. Just when she'd found her sister, she'd lost her. She did not want to lose Sarah's children, too.

She'd learned through the years that outward appearance didn't necessarily reflect a person's inner qualities, or lack of them. She was wearing mourning clothes, but Jonas was the one grieving.

Maybe, just maybe, she could take away some of his burden. His smile did not reach his eyes — eyes that she remembered as being a soft brown now looked like they were troubled by a dark rain cloud.

His smile now gone, he nodded. "Molly." He reached for her bag. "Thank you for coming."

She didn't want to show her disappointment that the children weren't with him.

She relinquished the bag and walked beside him toward the wagon. "Jonas, I — I have trunks."

"Trunks?"

The way he said it, it sounded as if he'd never heard the word before. "Yes. My clothes . . . and things."

His rugged face reddened. "Of — of course." He set the bag in the wagon. "Here." He held out his hand. Molly laid her shoulder bag on the seat and placed her gloved hand in his strong one. She hoisted her skirt to her ankles and stepped up.

Jonas hurried around to the other side, jumped up beside her, and picked up the reins. "I'll drive closer," he said. "Your trunks may be heavy."

He turned the wagon, and the horse trotted down to the luggage cart. Molly tried to reason why he seemed so somber.

She chided herself. Of course he was somber. He was grieving for his wife. He was a proud man who had to ask for help. She was dressed in black. He would expect her to be grieving and likely thought it wouldn't be proper to seem happy at such a distressing time.

She would swallow her excitement and act the proper mourning lady. At least until she could get out of those dismal clothes.

During her brief visits, she had never conversed with Jonas very much. When Percy came, he stayed in town at the hotel in Poplar Grove and Jonas slept in the lean-to. That way, Molly shared Sarah's bed and the two of them talked until the wee hours of the morning. Trying to sleep would have been a nuisance when they had so much to talk about. Sleep was for when they were no longer together.

Jonas had always been polite but reticent. Molly understood that. She'd learned to be exactly that with Percy. She observed Jonas being kind to Sarah and the children. But it was from Sarah that she'd gotten the impression Jonas was a remarkable man.

Sarah hadn't explained in what way he

was remarkable.

"I thought the children might be with you," she said as they pulled away from the depot.

She watched his chest rise slightly, but maybe that was from flicking the reins and giving the horse a command to pick up speed. "No," he said. "I, um, didn't think it fitting."

"Oh." Molly supposed he meant because they were grieving. His next words seemed to confirm her thoughts.

"I'm sorry I couldn't get away for Mr. Pierpont's funeral."

"Oh, I understand." She did exactly. He had children to take care of. He might have felt out of place, too, the funeral being a rather extraordinary event, unlike Sarah's simple one. "I'm just so glad you asked me to come and help."

He nodded. "I hope I wasn't imposing by asking such. I just had nowhere else to turn."

His words sounded like he considered her not a loving aunt to his children, but a last resort. His next comment surprised her even more.

"You may not be here long enough to wear all those clothes." His head jerked toward the trunks, then back at the winding dirt road ahead of them. "Dawn's arm should heal within a few weeks."

Molly opened her mouth to respond, but her glance at his concerned face caused her to close it. Was he hoping she wouldn't stay? She knew he and Percy hadn't cared much for each other, but she hadn't thought that extended to her.

For a long moment, she gazed at his set face. She knew about acting and remaining silent. However, no one could stop the thoughts she allowed to roam about in her head.

For years, she'd wanted to do something useful and now was her chance. No one else but Sarah had recognized the longing in her heart to be part of a real family.

She longed to give love to a young girl and little boy who had lost their mama. Molly knew how that felt because she'd lost her mama when she was eight years old. In a sense, soon after that, she'd lost her dad and sister, too.

Now Jonas, Dawn, and Caleb needed her. As much as she regretted that Dawn had broken her arm, she thought Jonas would otherwise never have consented to her coming to his home in Pine Hollow.

She would like to stay in this mountain cove permanently.

Her sister's children needed her and liked her.

She resolved, right then and there, that Jonas McLean, too, would learn to like her.

TWO

Molly's "Oops" brought his glance around to her. With one hand, she braced herself on the wooden seat and with the other she secured her hat on her head. Try as he might, Jonas was unable to avoid the wagon wheels dropping right down into the wide mud hole in the dirt road.

She swayed when the front wheels found level ground and the back wheels dipped into the hole.

"Sorry. Spring rains do this to dirt roads." His body rose a couple of inches into the air before settling back onto the seat.

The force of her laughter near his ear so startled him, he almost dropped the reins.

There had been none in his life since Sarah died. He and Sarah would have laughed about this, but it didn't seem fitting with someone else.

Molly's glance swept past his face and she gestured behind her. "At least the trunks are still there."

Jonas barely concentrated on her story of when she and Sarah were little girls in the back of her papa's wagon. The roads weren't even this good and they'd bounce up and down like rubber balls.

He couldn't manage more than a forced turn of his lips. He and Sarah had many happy times in their marriage. But he couldn't remember any of them without that insatiable longing rising up within him. Now, hearing Molly's laughter, he felt her loss of a sister didn't come close to his loss of a wife, or his children's loss of a mother.

She faced the front again. "I remember those mud holes. I've even played in a few."

Watching the road ahead for more holes to try to avoid, he spoke honestly. "Everything's different, being an adult. When you're responsible for a family."

"Oh, I know how hard it must be for you, Jonas, without . . ." He heard the catch in her voice. "Without Sarah."

He could only nod. Did she really know? Had she loved Percival Pierpont the way he loved Sarah? "I have to think about the children, Molly. This is hard on them."

From the corner of his eye, he saw her turn slightly toward him. "Jonas, you can't imagine what it means to me that you asked me to come here."

He swallowed hard. "Sarah made me promise to ask you for help if anything ever happened to her."

Molly turned toward the front again. He glimpsed the movement of her gloves against each other as if she didn't know what to do with her hands. Maybe she thought he didn't appreciate her willingness to help. He did. He had asked her because he had nowhere else to turn. He could at least be kind.

"I do thank you for coming, Molly. But life here is different than in the . . ." They both lifted from their seats again as a wheel bumped through another hole. He said, "city," while she emitted a small sound of glee.

Sarah had been quick to laugh, too. She'd packed joy into every day's living, as if — as if she knew her life would be short. Somehow, Molly's laughter seemed out of place, considering the situation. She'd lost her husband only three months ago. She was wearing black. And yet, she was behaving as if she were about to see Sarah again and experience those happy times when she'd visited.

He and the children didn't need someone to pretend everything was all right. Molly had lived a pampered city life. Maybe she didn't realize what she was getting into. He took in a deep breath. "Visits aren't the same as daily living, Molly."

Without looking around, he knew her head had turned sharply toward him. His mere glance to the side revealed her smile had vanished and her chin had lifted, reminding him of how Dawn often looked when things didn't go her way. Sarah said their daughter got her hardheadedness from him, but he suspected it ran in Sarah's family.

A wave of remorse swept over him. He forced it away. He didn't have the luxury of spending time thinking about what couldn't be. He had two children to raise and didn't know how he could do it without their mother.

If he didn't know, how could she?

At least, he should warn her about his daughter.

"About Dawn —"

"Oh, that adorable child. I can't wait to see her. Jonas, this is just what I need." She gasped, then whispered, "Listen."

He listened but heard nothing other than the *clop-clop* of the horse's hooves and churning of wagon wheels on a rough road. Had she heard a wild animal? Wouldn't surprise him to see a bear with her cubs, deer, or even a bobcat.

He shrugged a shoulder.

"The birds." She pointed toward the trees where a flock of birds flew and twittered. "You're so right, Jonas. This is different from the city. We don't see that many birds. Our spring is pretty, of course. But here there is so much more abundance. I mean, look at the colors."

He hadn't noticed. His world was a cold, gray one. He looked at the delight on her face — the face that held a resemblance to Sarah, and yet was so different — as different as the city from the mountains. He marveled, almost resented, her describing the colors of red maple buds; pink, purple, and white rhododendron; delicate mountain laurel; new leaves on tall oaks; and the yellow-green poplar flowers that resembled tulips. She laughed lightly and turned her face toward him. "And . . . springy-green growth on towering pines."

Jonas looked, but the colors of spring didn't seem to register. His heart felt cold like winter and black as the coal the miners took from the Black Mountains.

He'd heard people say that winter seemed endless back in the hollows. Now he knew what that meant — and it had nothing to do with weather or a season.

Molly was wearing black, but he was the one feeling the blackness. Maybe she looked upon this as a long visit. He was the one who had a lifelong responsibility.

He decided not to say that Dawn was not the same little girl she'd been when Molly had visited. Dawn had more than a broken arm. She had a broken heart and a broken spirit.

Molly reveled in the changing sights as the wagon made its circuitous route around the Piney Mountains. Craggy peaks and forested slopes rose to over four thousand feet above sea level. Cascading waterfalls rushed over smooth boulders, splashing and rippling along creeks. The fresh smell of water mingled with rich soil.

Orange lilies along the roadsides waved in welcome. Red-crested songbirds greeted. The wagon moved past men building a dirt road off the main road. Yellow daffodils and delicate pastel narcissus grew beside a fence.

Rather than continue talking to this man, whose grief seemed so heavy he couldn't respond with more than a few words, she breathed in the fragrance of mountain-fresh air, spring flowers, and spicy pine.

After a few more miles up and along the

winding road, Jonas turned onto his wooded land in Pine Hollow. Soon, they rode out of the trees and ahead was a sight that made her heart leap with joy. The small valley stretched out ahead — land she'd seen in the past that had corn as high as a man's head, beans that formed a blanket of green, wildflowers that grew freely, grassy stretches of pasture where cattle fed — then the forested mountains reaching into the sky.

Oh, how she preferred that to a trolley car running on rails down the middle of a cobbled city street. She loved the natural beauty here, away from any man-made contraptions.

Molly began to feel like Jonas looked when the log cabin came into view. A churning in her stomach made her feel sick and a tightness in her throat kept her from speaking. Her determination to think only of the good, of coming home again, left her. She fought against moisture in her eyes and breathed deeply.

No Sarah ran out to meet her.

In front of the cabin, no spring flowers bloomed in the bed, except a few jonquils struggling to survive in the weeds.

A dread hammered in her chest as it had when they'd lowered Sarah's coffin into the ground. Dawn had begged them not to cover her mother with dirt. When they did it anyway, she'd run back to the cabin and wouldn't come out of her room.

Molly's gaze moved up and away, to the distant hills, beyond which Sarah lay beneath the earth in a pine coffin. For the first time since Jonas asked her to help, she had her doubts. Could she do this?

Hearing the creak of a door, the name "Sarah" sounded from her throat in a whisper. She looked quickly at Jonas. He appeared not to hear but stared at the cabin.

When the cabin door swung open, Molly expected Dawn would run out, followed by a toddling Caleb. Instead, a stocky woman with her shirtwaist sleeves rolled to above her elbows, rushed into the yard, brushing back some of the hair that had come loose from the roll at the back of her neck.

Jonas walked up, looking concerned. "The children?"

"They'll be right out," she said. "I'm sure." She didn't sound sure.

Jonas nodded, although he didn't look too sure of anything, either. "Molly, you may remember Birdie Evers, the pastor's wife."

Molly had met her nine months before at Sarah's funeral. She recognized her mainly as the woman who had one completely gray streak along the right side of her black hair.

Molly extended her gloved hand. "Nice to see you again, Mrs. Evers."

The woman wiped her hands on her apron covering her long, gray skirt, ignored Molly's hand, then opened her arms and gathered Molly against her ample chest. "Oh, my dear." She began expressing her sorrow for all Molly's losses. "I'm glad you're here."

She moved back. "Now, you call me by my front name. It's Birdie. Everybody does."

Molly wondered if that was her name, or a nickname because of the movement of her hands when she talked, and equally darting black eyes that gave her the appearance of being all aflutter.

Molly smiled. She sent a quick glance toward the house while Jonas set her bag next to her, then returned to the wagon.

Birdie clasped her hands then unclasped them and yelled at Jonas. "Let me help you with that, Jonas. You'll break your back."

She rushed to the wagon and seemed to have less trouble than Jonas with the heavy trunks.

Birdie brushed her hands together like someone playing the cymbals. "There. Now let me help you inside with them."

"The porch will be fine," Jonas said.

Molly felt planted in the yard. Why did he unload her trunks here? Where were the children? Napping? Maybe someone else was coming to load her trunks. "Why didn't you leave the trunks in the wagon?"

Jonas stared back. "What do you mean? You've already decided not to stay?"

Molly's thoughts were all a-jumble. Jonas and Birdie wore expressions of confusion. Molly thought he would have arranged for her to stay with someone who had an extra room and she'd come to the cabin during the day.

"Of course I'm planning to stay," she stammered.

He looked over his shoulder at the trunks, then back at her. "I don't understand why you're asking about the trunks. This is my home."

Figuring she'd just make things worse by trying to explain, she shook her head. "Never mind." She touched the side of her head. "Must be the mountain air."

Birdie looked from one to another with raised eyebrows and a quirk of her lips that seemed to say she was enjoying this. Her nose squeezed together and she inhaled deeply, then spread her hands. "Well, I should be leaving."

"Thank you, Birdie," Jonas said. "I appreciate your help."

Her hand lifted in a wave. "Bye-bye,

Molly. Call on me if you need anything. I'm just across yonder creek and up a few miles."

Molly didn't see a yonder creek but watched Birdie stride across the yard to a horse tied to a tree limb. The woman, now obviously wearing a divided skirt, mounted the horse and disappeared around the side of the cabin.

Molly turned back.

Jonas still stared at her. "Did you forget I live here?"

"No, no." She knew he had only two bedrooms. "I just didn't think we'd be — I'd be — staying in the same house with — you."

If she didn't know better she would think he'd been working out in the sun all day, the way color flooded his cheeks. "It wouldn't be proper for us to stay in the same house together."

She felt reprimanded, as if she had suggested such. Now, she felt like the one who'd worked all day in the sun.

He explained further. "You'll have my room. I will be in the lean-to at the barn."

She opened her mouth to say she didn't want to put him out of his house, but that might sound even less proper and he'd probably send her back to the city before her trunks could get through the front door of his cabin.

About the time she again remembered the children, she heard their voices.

"You stay right here!"

"Wanna go."

"No. She's not your mama. We don't have no mama no more."

Molly stared. Dawn, with her arm in a splint and sling tried to hold a squirming little boy with one hand. He broke loose and ran straight to Molly.

With his little arms around her legs he looked up into her eyes with a hopeful face. "Mama?"

Jonas took hold of the boy's shoulder. "Caleb," he said in a reprimanding tone.

Molly looked over at him. "It's all right."

Caleb was so young when his mama died. But old enough to know he had one. Molly knelt down to the little boy's level. "I'm your Aunt Molly, Caleb. I'm here for a visit until Dawn's arm is healed."

His little lips quivered and he looked disappointed. Molly patted her bag. "I have something in here you might like."

Caleb took in a deep breath and let it out in a rush, as if he'd been told to be brave and not cry. He nodded and she stood, picking up her bag. Caleb reached for her hand. The two of them walked to the screen door.

Dawn slammed the wooden one in her face.

THREE

Jonas opened the door Dawn had slammed. Although his heart hurt for his little girl, he'd have to reprimand her for such bad behavior. Caleb and Molly held the screen door open while Jonas dragged the trunks across the hardwood floor of the front room.

"Oh," Molly said, coming into the room. "You've divided the rooms."

He'd done that during the winter. It's something Sarah had wanted so she could entertain visitors without always taking them into the kitchen. He didn't know if that was something Molly had put into Sarah's head or if he'd done it himself by describing city homes that had large living rooms, dining rooms, and kitchens, all separate.

He dragged one of the trunks toward the bedroom. "Sarah wanted the rooms separate after we got the new cookstove." He felt a pang of regret that Sarah never got to see the finished room. So many things they discussed never came to fruition. He'd thought they had all the time in the world.

He looked up from his bent-over position when Caleb pulled on Molly's skirt and asked if she brought "canny."

Molly smiled down at Caleb. "You remember Aunt Molly bringing you candy?"

A dimple dented his cheek. His cotton-top head bobbed up and down.

"Well, I've heard your mama say that you can't have candy until after supper. Remember that?"

He clamped his lips tightly together, looked from side to side, and shook his head. Molly laughed and rubbed her hand across the top of his hair that was already rumpled and falling down over his forehead. "I'll bet you'll be ready for supper before long. Want to show me the kitchen?"

"Uh-huh." He reached for her hand.

"Yes, ma'am," Jonas corrected.

Caleb looked up at Molly with big, soulful blue eyes, the color of Sarah's, the color of Molly's.

Jonas knew Molly was trying to relate, but Dawn should be the one showing Molly the kitchen and where to find things.

He dragged the trunk into his bedroom, then came out and walked down to the closed door of the children's room. He thumped on it with the side of his fist. "Dawn, come out."

He waited.

She didn't.

He opened the door. Dawn sat on the floor at her window, looking out.

"Dawn."

She glanced over her shoulder with a defiant look then turned away.

"You come out right now and behave yourself. We have a guest. You know how to act."

Her only movement was a shrug.

"You mind me now, Dawn. Come out and show your Aunt Molly the kitchen."

"She's seen it before."

Jonas had never had to deal with this kind of behavior from her. He tried to keep his voice calm. "She hasn't seen it from the viewpoint of a cook."

Dawn stood and walked past him with downcast eyes. She walked ahead of Molly as she and Caleb followed. His daughter, who seemed like a stranger now, stopped at the doorway and gestured. "There it is." She returned to her room and shut the door.

Jonas tried to apologize. "I've never seen her act this way."

"I understand," Molly said and glanced at

Caleb as if she didn't want to say too much in front of him. "I'm sure it's hard for a child to deal with a broken arm. Maybe later she will feel more like showing me the kitchen, along with Caleb. I could go ahead and unpack a few things."

He dragged the other trunk into the bedroom. Caleb followed Molly, looking her over with a mixture of curiosity and admiration.

Jonas apologized again when he took his few work clothes from the chest and realized Sarah's clothes were still in the closet and stacked in drawers. Molly said she would take care of them.

Dawn might be the one who was right in this situation. Molly was not her mama. Jonas was moving out. Sarah's things would be stored away. Molly would sleep in the bed where he and Sarah had slept. Was this right?

Should he have sent Dawn and Caleb to the city until Dawn's arm healed? But that wouldn't have been reasonable with Dawn's having a broken arm and being on medication. He had to stop thinking about what might have been and concentrate on what was. "I'll take my Sunday clothes to the children's closet. Wouldn't seem right being in church smelling like a cow or a horse."

Soon as he said it, he realized some did smell like their animals.

"That's fine. Now, Jonas, would you like to see the presents I brought for the children?"

They left the bedroom. He started to set his stack of clothes on the sofa, then thought better of it. "I'll see them after I carry these out and take care of the horse."

Molly nodded. "Maybe Dawn will join us then."

"She will come out now," he said, pretending he had control of this situation. He thumped on Dawn's door with the side of his fist. "Young lady. Come out of there right now."

He held his breath for a couple of seconds. Suppose she didn't come out? She didn't need a spanking or harsh words. But she didn't need to be holed up in her room, either. They had to get through this somehow.

In the past, Dawn had been as eager for Molly to visit as Sarah had been. They had looked forward to Molly's laughter, presents, and talk about city life. Surely Dawn had not forgotten that.

He opened the door and almost immediately Dawn came up to him. She stood like a sad little statue, staring at the floor. He wanted to take her in his arms and cry and say he knew — he knew. Her comfort had been in taking care of him after Sarah died. Sarah had taught her to cook many things. She swept and dusted and even had Caleb help with some chores until she broke her arm.

She stifled her emotions, like he had to do. "You were rude to your aunt Molly who has come to help out. I want you to apologize and behave yourself."

She obeyed, but it was obvious her heart wasn't in it. She spoke to the floor. "Sorry."

"It's all right," Molly said. "Now, maybe you and Caleb can show me where everything is in the kitchen. After your papa comes back, you can have your presents."

Jonas took a deep breath when he walked out onto the back porch. Caleb took to Molly. That was good. But set against Dawn's hostility, was that good enough? And was it good for Caleb?

"What's done is done, Jonas," he told himself while walking to the lean-to. He'd added this room for hired hands who sometimes needed to stay overnight during harvest season.

Now, he'd be living like a hired hand.

He sat on the bunk and with elbows on his thighs, put his hands over his face, and bent forward. "Lord, I'm at a loss here. I don't know what's right anymore. Sometimes I feel like I'm two people being pulled in opposite directions. Most times I feel like half a person without my Sarah."

He raised his head and looked at the wooden-beamed ceiling, seeking answers. What he saw were dusty cobwebs.

He went out to bring his wagon into the barn and unhitch Mac. When Dawn was a toddler she had inadvertently named the horse after hearing the lyrics in "Yankee Doodle" about a man who went to town on a pony, stuck a feather in his hat, then called it macaroni. She'd gleefully called their foal "Mac-a-pony." Jonas and Sarah had laughed until they cried. "Mac the pony" was fitting for the McLeans' youngest horse.

At least in the barn he had something alive to talk to. "Okay, Mac. This is not forever. It's only for a few weeks — if she stays that long. I'll find someone from the mission house or an older woman who doesn't remind the children of Sarah. But it's good to have someone to take care of Caleb and do the cooking."

Mac snorted, and Jonas didn't know if that was agreement or not.

After a few weeks Jonas could return to his house. Molly could return to the city, and he would appreciate her help of occasionally sending a dress for his daughter or some other feminine things. That's probably what Sarah had in mind anyway. Isn't that what aunts did for their nieces?

In the meantime, he needed to see what gifts their aunt had brought. Maybe that would bring a smile to the face of his young daughter who hadn't smiled in a long time.

Molly pretended she didn't notice that Dawn sat in a chair at the table, unresponsive to what was going on. At least the young girl was going through the motions. Sometimes that's all a person could do. She knew.

Caleb opened a cabinet door. "A pot for corn."

"A pot for . . . um . . . beans."

Caleb pointed to a pan. "A pot for . . . eggs." He looked up. "And chicken." He made a chewing motion with his lips. "Mmmmm."

Delight bubbled up inside Molly. Caleb was trying so hard to please her. Yes, he needed her. So did Dawn, although she didn't know it. "Maybe we could have chicken for supper."

He nodded. "An' canny."

"Yes, you little scamp." She rumpled his

hair again and his blue eyes shone. She knew he was more hungry for a woman's touch than for food. Molly wanted to shower him with affection, but she'd have to be careful. She needed his love and acceptance, too. How to give and accept that without driving a deep wedge between the boy and his sister, she didn't know.

Caleb opened a drawer. "A-p'ons," he explained.

"I'll wear one of those while I cook supper."

For an instant she let her hand rest on the soft fabric. Sarah had worn this. She unfolded it and was about to slip it on.

Dawn's voice stopped her. "That's my mama's apron."

Caleb gave his sister a mean look, then touched the apron. "You can have it."

"No, she can't. It's Mama's."

Molly's gaze shifted to Dawn, and her heart went out to the sad-faced little girl. "You're right, Dawn. This is a beautiful apron. Did your mama make it?"

Dawn's nostrils flared slightly. She averted her gaze. "Yes."

Molly pretended not to notice Dawn's distant attitude. She refolded the apron and returned it to the drawer. "I'm sure your mama would want you to wear it someday in your own kitchen."

Dawn said, "This is my own kitchen."

"Dawn!"

Molly breathed a sigh of relief to see Jonas standing in the doorway. She didn't know how long she could keep from taking the little girl by the shoulders, looking her in the eye, and telling her she knew exactly how she felt. But this was not the time, and that was not the way. Molly wanted to love her — did love her — and it hurt not to have that love accepted.

Caleb yelled, "P'esents! P'esents!" easing the tension.

He ran into the front room, took hold of the handle of the bag, and tugged, scooting it a little closer to Molly.

Molly picked it up, went over to the couch and sat down, then opened it. She took out a package wrapped in paper and held it out to Dawn, who stood against the door casing.

When Jonas cleared his throat loudly, Dawn walked over and took it. She sat in a chair and unwrapped it. She stared at the porcelain doll.

Jonas prompted, "What do you say, Dawn?"

She responded blandly. "Thank you."

"You're welcome." Molly had planned to

tell Dawn she chose that doll because it reminded her of Dawn with its brown hair with golden highlights and light brown eyes. The doll reminded Molly of a Victorian princess in silk, adorned with lace and seed pearls and she carried her own little parasol.

Molly decided not to mention the dress for Dawn and outfit for Caleb that were in her trunk. She knew from experience that toys and dresses didn't mean much when your heart was breaking.

"My p'esent now," Caleb said.

"Oh, you want a doll, too?"

He screwed up his nose and shook his head.

Molly laughed and took out three small boxes. Caleb jerked off the top of one. "Ohhhh." He took out a train car.

Jonas leaned forward. This interested him more than the doll. Dawn stared at the boxes. Maybe she would have preferred a train.

Caleb jerked off the other lids. Jonas explained that one was an engine and the one painted red was a caboose.

"Ca-booze," Caleb repeated and laughed.

Jonas sat on the floor and hooked them together, then Caleb took off with them across the floor. Molly thought that small turn of Jonas's lips might be a smile.

She had a present for him, but this wasn't the time.

"Well," she said. "Caleb wants chicken for supper. What about you two?"

Dawn remained silent.

Jonas spoke. "Sounds good to me."

Molly cleared her throat. "Um. Jonas, do you want to do the honors. I mean" — she winced — "chop off the head?"

She heard a groan from Dawn, but Jonas said, "Sure thing."

"And where do you keep your milk?"

This time Molly preferred that Dawn remain silent. But the girl spoke up. "The milk is in the cow."

FOUR

Jonas wasn't sure how to pray. He hadn't been sure for a long time. It wasn't that he blamed God for Sarah's death. He knew life was hard and people died. But during the past nine months he just didn't know how to face it all with a positive attitude.

He sat at the head of the table, trying to ignore the odor left over from the pan of grease catching fire. "Let us pray."

Caleb folded his hands beneath his chin. They all bowed their heads.

Jonas began. "Lord, we come to You needing Your help. You've blessed us real good and put a meal on our table. Especially, we want to thank You for Molly coming to help us out for a while. Bless this food and may it help us be strong. Amen."

Molly looked over at Caleb, who'd insisted he sit beside her.

He smiled at her. "I want a egg, p'ease."

Seeing Molly's surprise, Jonas quickly

explained. "His favorite piece of chicken is the leg."

Apparently realizing Caleb wasn't too articulate with his *L*s, Molly's expression relaxed. She forked a chicken leg and laid it on Caleb's plate.

"Thank you."

He was being particularly polite, obviously wanting to please Molly. He needed a mother figure, but he'd lose it again when Molly left. For now, however, Jonas would accept about anything to distract his children from their loss.

Molly forked her chicken and held the plate out to Dawn.

Dawn took hers and curled her lip. "It's burnt."

Jonas didn't know how his sweet little girl could have become so vindictive. On second thought, he did. Although he knew better, he'd done his share of taking his frustration and loss out on a bale of hay he'd pitchforked into the barn. He'd given his cow and horse an earful while shoveling out the waste.

Caleb had openly cried for his mama. Jonas had been able to hold him and soothe his grief while his own tears wet his cheeks. Dawn had withdrawn and remained quiet, except at night when he heard her cry into her pillow.

But that didn't mean she could be disrespectful to Molly, no matter how burnt the supper might be. "It's just a little brown. I . . ." He cleared his throat. "I like it that way." It wasn't exactly a lie. He'd had no lunch, was hungry, and a raw chicken might taste good at this point. Since the grease caught fire, there was no gravy, but the mashed potatoes were good. Lumps were still potatoes. He was thankful there wasn't much one could do to ruin green beans taken from a jar.

Dawn's slow movement of her eyes toward him said plain as day she knew that wasn't the most truthful thing he'd ever said.

"I have done better," Molly admitted. "I just have to get used to the woodstove."

Caleb confirmed that Molly could do no wrong. "I wike it aww," he said. But after a few minutes he said he was full. "Can I pway with my twain?"

"After you clean up your plate," Jonas said. He decided to steer the conversation to city life just to have Molly talk and the children listen. He should make an effort to involve her, act interested, and make her feel a part of things. "Um, Molly, you went to the city to live with your aunt and uncle when you were around Dawn's age, right?"

45

"A year younger." She picked at the dark crust on her piece of chicken that looked rather dry. Apparently, casual conversation wasn't going to be easy.

"Dawn," he said, "wouldn't you like to know what the schools are like in the city?"

She shook her head. "No. I don't like the city."

"You've never been there."

"I've heard about it. I don't like it. I like right here."

He felt apologetic and addressed Molly. "After your visits, Dawn would ask all sorts of questions about city life." He took a bite of chicken. The inside was fine, and he didn't want to insult Molly by peeling off the burnt crust.

Molly took a sip of milk, lifted her chin, and smiled. She began talking about the city as if nothing were amiss. "The schools have several classrooms and many teachers. Most people have small gardens, but they don't have to. They can choose to grow their own food or go to a store and buy it. There's the butcher shop where you can buy all kinds of meat. And there are grocery stores that sell vegetables and fruit. We can even have ice for our drinks and eat ice cream."

Dawn spoke up. "We don't have to go to the city for ice cream. I had some in town."

Molly's eyes brightened. "Oh, don't you just love it?"

Dawn shrugged. "It's okay."

Jonas studied his daughter. She had been excited about eating an ice cream sundae at the store in Poplar Grove. She had told her friends and discussed many times that she had vanilla ice cream with chocolate syrup, nuts, and a cherry on top.

Glancing at Molly, he saw the look of defeat in her eyes before she turned her attention on the one she could count on for a positive response. "Did you have ice cream, Caleb?"

His lower lip poked out and he shook his head, giving her that poor-little-hound-dog look.

Molly laughed. "We'll just have to do something about that."

Dawn piped up. "Don't take him to the city for that. He can get it in town."

Jonas both admired and sympathized with Molly's trying to draw Dawn into the conversation. She asked about school, friends, and interests and Dawn's replies consisted of "Yes, ma'am; No, ma'am; Don't remember," or a shrug.

Finally, Molly gave up and addressed her questions to Jonas. "Could you teach me to milk a cow?" She laughed. "I'm not sure

47

I'm ready for . . ." Her gaze settled on the chicken plate. "For . . . some things."

He figured she meant chopping off a chicken's head.

At least she wasn't overly sensitive about her ineptness as to their way of life. He wasn't exactly the greatest in the kitchen himself. "Sure," he said. "Dawn and I will clean up after supper while you get unpacked. Then we can have a milking lesson."

After supper, he delighted in watching Caleb, not listlessly playing at something, but enjoying the train and even making *choo-choo, chug-chug,* and whistle sounds.

Jonas had wanted to talk with Dawn. He washed a plate with the dishrag and laid it in the rinse water. "Are you trying to hurt your aunt's feelings, Dawn?"

"No." She swished the plate around in the water, shook it, and laid it on a towel. Her face turned toward him with a sincere expression. "I liked her visiting us, Pa. But she don't belong here now. Mama said I was s'pose to take care of you and Caleb."

"She didn't mean you were supposed to do all that she did. You're still a child, Dawn. You need to . . ."

What did she need to do? Have fun? Not do adult things?

She shook another plate and laid it aside. "Nothing's fun anymore. And Caleb's acting like she's his mama. That's not right. He shouldn't forget Mama."

Forget. If only Jonas could for one waking moment, maybe life would be easier. "Caleb needs Molly right now."

Her voice quivered. "If I hadn't broke my arm, he wouldn't."

If.

A lot of things would be different, if . . .

"We can't change what is, Dawn. We just have to do the best we can. The good Lord will get us through this. Can you be the sweet little girl I know you are to your aunt Molly?"

Dawn's hand stilled in the water. She didn't seem to be a child when she raised her head and looked through the window over the sink. Her words echoed what he so often felt deep inside. "I don't know."

Surely not!

Was she really supposed to do *that?*

Molly felt more aversion to touching a cow's underside than at the thought of chopping off a chicken's head.

Was she good for nothing, as Dawn's every look implied?

Jonas likely thought so, too.

49

At least Caleb, accompanied by a couple of hounds, was having fun finding rocks to put in his train car. Was there nothing else positive about her being here? Would there ever be?

While Jonas and Dawn cleaned up the kitchen, she had unpacked a few more things and laid out some dresses that needed ironing. Then it was time for her milking lesson.

Dawn called the cow into the barn, and Jonas set a pail under the animal. With her foot, Dawn scooted a stool up to the pail.

Jonas gave his first instruction. "Just don't get too close to the hind legs. Cows can kick."

Having no idea in how many directions the cow could kick, Molly moved the stool to midway of the cow, wondering if she had to crawl under there. Observing the knee joints of the cow, she figured the front legs kicked backward.

Dawn huffed. "You need to be close to the udder."

With open mouth, Molly stared at Jonas. Would he allow his young daughter to say such a word? He didn't react except to move the stool closer to it and sat down. "Here's how you do it."

She watched and heard the *squirt, squirt,*

squirt of milk streaming into the pail. A big gray cat appeared, obviously accustomed to the stream of milk Jonas directed its way. Then the cat obeyed his, "Scat."

He stood. "Just squeeze and pull."

Rather than let him stare at her burning face, she sat. She reached out a hand, almost touched it but drew back.

Dawn snickered.

Jonas's eyes warned Dawn, but his dimple, like Caleb's, indicated he was stifling a laugh.

"Go outside and tend to Caleb," Jonas said to Dawn.

Molly wanted to tell Dawn her eyes might get stuck if she kept rolling them up toward the sky like that. Instead, she faced the cow's side. Determined, she reached one hand out and grabbed.

"Both hands," he said.

She did, but groaned. "This is much too personal."

"It's just a cow who's going to get mighty grumpy if she's not milked. Now pump."

Pump!

Angry with him and herself, and the stinky cow in a musty barn smelling of odors she didn't want to think about, she tightened her grip and jerked. The cow protested, and she screamed.

She got a face-full and a dress-dousing at the same time. Coming from Jonas was the strangest-sounding throat clearing she'd ever heard. About ready to tackle a man instead of a cow, she jumped up and faced him, swiping her face with her hand and dried it on the side of her dress.

The look on his face was strange, too, but something about the way his brow furrowed and his gentle tone when he said, "You're supposed to aim at the bucket," eased her frustration somewhat. She felt like running out, but facing Dawn would be an added humiliation.

He sat on the stool and started pumping. Milk flowed freely into the pail. Molly marveled at that. Maybe the cow didn't like her either.

"That was fine for a first lesson," he said. "You need strong hands for this. That will come with practice."

What she needed more was a strong stomach and an iron will. She wasn't sure that would come. She watched until he finished the milking, then they walked outside.

"I see we got milk," Dawn said.

"Of course," Molly retorted as if she had done it, even though she suspected Dawn had peeked into the barn and knew who did the milking.

"I'll put the children to bed," Jonas said.

"Do you want me to bathe Caleb?"

"No, I'll wash him off."

"Tell your aunt Molly good night."

Molly knelt down, and Caleb hugged her.

She kissed his cheek and told him good night. In a fast getaway, Dawn had already reached the cabin.

Molly felt close to tears. She walked across the backyard, past the wooden swing hanging from a long rope tied to a branch of the big oak. She'd just had her first lesson in milking, and it was as big a disaster as the grease fire. At least she'd known to throw flour on the fire — the flour she'd planned to use for gravy.

Now she looked like she'd made gravy on her clothes after the milk combined with the dusting of flour on her black dress. She'd seen plenty of cows in her childhood but had never milked one. Her papa had done that chore.

Something seemed to catch in her throat at the thought of him. She'd never quite forgiven him for what he did. But she missed him. And Sarah.

Her gaze moved to the fields — some showing evidence of early planting, others waiting to be plowed — and to the grazing field for the horse and cow. The occasional mooing of cattle and the horse's whinny were replaced by insects coming out and having a party of their own, accompanied by the baying of a distant hound.

A silvery moon made an arc in the graying sky. A few twinkling stars appeared. Gray twilight began settling over the landscape.

Looking at the approaching darkness was like looking at her life. How quickly her concept of it had changed in a moment. She was to come here, be loved and accepted, then like in a fairy tale, live happily ever after.

She should have known better. She'd believed in fairy tales when she was a child, and they never came true. She was a mature woman of twenty-four now and needed to face facts. Jonas asked her here only because he had nowhere else to turn. Dawn resented her. Caleb wanted her to be his mama, which meant he had another heartache in store.

But she couldn't leave her sister's family when they needed someone. She crossed her arms and hugged them when a sudden gust of cool air swept over her.

"There you are," she heard from behind.

She blinked away any moisture that the wind must have brought to her eyes and turned her face toward Jonas as he walked up. "The children asleep?"

"Caleb can hardly keep his eyes open. He doesn't want the lamp out before he goes to sleep. He wasn't that way before. . . ."

Molly realized Jonas had a hard time talking about Sarah. He looked into the distance. "Dawn's reading to him. She's allowed to stay awake longer, so she reads."

A slight hope surfaced that she might be able to reach Dawn through the books she'd brought from the city.

Her thoughts returned to Jonas when he said, "Sorry about the dress." His lips tightened, and his brow wrinkled. Apparently, Jonas wasn't about to laugh about anything, even if he thought it funny.

"I'll just throw it away. I don't like wearing black. I did it for appearance."

His surprised look made her realize he didn't understand. He couldn't, and this wasn't the time to explain it. Wearing black for her deceased husband seemed a mockery, like living a lie. Much of her life had been like living a lie. She'd hoped to escape that.

Maybe it wasn't possible.

"Oh, Jonas. I don't mean to make light of

anyone's death. But, no matter what I wore, I mourned for Sarah over the past fifteen years."

After an extended thoughtful gaze, he nodded and glanced at the mess on her dress. "If you can't make anything out of the dress, you might tear it up for rags. We can always use cleaning cloths."

"Oh, I didn't think of that."

His voice was distant, sort of like the baying hound. "Well, you didn't need to in the city."

No, but her aunt's hired hands would have worn anything she discarded. But she didn't think it would sound right to ask if he knew any mountain woman who would want her milk-and flour-spattered, grease-stained mourning dress.

She should learn to be silent, like Dawn.

Only Sarah had seemed to enjoy whatever she had to say, no matter how foolish. And she'd been with Sarah so seldom. So seldom.

That reminded her of what she wanted to do. She reached into her pocket and drew out an item wrapped in a lacy handkerchief. She held it out. "I have a gift for you, Jonas."

His arm came up, bent at the wrist to ward her off as if she were a disease.

FIVE

"You don't need to give me any presents, Molly. Really, I —"

Many times, Molly had been admonished to be grateful for what she was given and to appreciate gifts.

Now she recalled that Sarah had said Jonas was afraid her presents would spoil her and the children. But Sarah had seemed to love the presents. Molly hadn't taken the remark seriously. She'd heard mothers say their children were spoiled, but they'd smiled like that was an attribute. Had Jonas not liked her giving presents? In the past, that had been all she had to offer.

She felt a tremor in her hand and hoped her voice wouldn't reveal such. "Just . . . take a look."

She placed the item in his open palm. He tentatively opened the folds of the white handkerchief. He turned the small picture frame over. He stared, as if seeing a ghost.

His face paled. "You — you did this?"

"No. I'm not an artist. You remember the photographer who was here, taking pictures after that mining accident and crowds gathered? Percy didn't like the man taking a picture of me and Sarah. The photographer promised to send the photograph to Percy. I've had it ever since."

"But . . . this is colored. . . ."

Looking fondly at the picture, Molly nodded. "After Sarah's death, I took the photograph to an artist. I had him paint Sarah's portrait and helped him choose the right colors for her face, hair, and eyes."

Jonas held the picture out to her. "It's . . . yours."

"No, Jonas. I did it for you. I have the black and white." He closed his eyes and swayed. The only thing she could think to say was, "It's oil."

He nodded. Night had come with a bright moonlight shining down upon them, making a silvery halo on his dark hair. He replaced the folds of the handkerchief over the frame.

His lips trembled. So did his voice when he whispered, "I don't have an image of her. Thank you." He choked out, "Good night, Molly."

The last thing Molly saw before looking

away were the moon-silvered streaks of wetness running down his cheeks.

The last thing he looked at before going to sleep was the little oil painting of Sarah in that pewter frame sitting on the crate beside the bunk. He whispered, "Good night, Sarah, my love," and turned the knob on the lamp. The flame went out, a thin trail of smoke disappeared in the darkness, leaving behind the faint odor of a burnt oil wick.

"That's my life now, Sarah." The slats creaked with the weight of his turning on his back. With open eyes, he felt the darkness, despite the moonlight shining through the windows. He closed his eyes against it and reminisced. His grandpa built that cabin, raised their son in it, and passed it down to Jonas. He and Sarah built a life there. That's where she birthed their children, the ones who'd lived and the ones who'd died. That's where she breathed her last.

So, what was he doing in the barn while a city woman slept in their bed?

He reckoned he really couldn't have stood it if Molly hadn't given him the painting of Sarah. He would have marched up there and said he and his children would find some way to make it without his leaving them with a citified aunt.

But that gift touched something deep in his heart and made him think maybe — maybe Molly could do some good here.

Maybe she did understand grieving more than he gave her credit for. What she said about black clothes made sense. He just wished he could remove that black covering that had wrapped its way around his heart and tear it up for rags. But it just lay there, without producing any warmth at all.

The first thing Jonas said after hearing the rooster crow was, "Good morning, Sarah." He picked up the picture but didn't need to turn it toward the early morning light to see it better. He saw Sarah. "I know you loved your sister. She's given me this gift. I have nothing to give her but my acceptance. I'm really going to try."

Later, Jonas reminded himself of his resolve to try when he came home for lunch. When plowing on a clear day like this, he usually took his lunch with him and didn't come home 'til dark. The situation being what it was, he thought it best to look in on things.

With all the ruckus going on, nobody noticed him riding up. Something terrible must have happened. Birdie Evers was there and they all were gathered around something. He heard Molly wailing, "Oh, I broke it. I broke it."

"Don't worry, child," Birdie said. "There's more than one way to kill a chicken." Birdie picked up the staggering chicken with its head hanging to one side. After one terrific swing of her arm in a circle, the chicken's head was in Birdie's hand, dripping blood, while the body flopped all over the yard.

Molly wailed. "It's hurt. It's hurt."

"That's reflex," Birdie said. She held up its bloody head. "You don't hear it cackling, do you?"

Molly's hand went to her heart and she paled, moaning.

Birdie chuckled while Caleb, with his arms outstretched in front of him, ran around chasing the flopping chicken body.

Molly moaned. "I don't know if I'll ever eat another chicken."

"That's what the good Lord made them for."

Jonas tied his horse and walked closer. Dawn saw him first. She had that disgusted look on her face, shook her head, and rolled her eyes toward heaven. She walked over to him and spoke loudly enough for all to hear this time. "We had chicken last night."

Molly looked helpless. "Well . . . there's

nothing else."

"Sure there is," Jonas said. "Didn't Dawn show you the canned meat? We also have cured meat in the cellar."

Dawn turned and ran off across the yard, past where the cow was grazing and up to the top of a hill. Jonas didn't try to stop her.

Birdie seemed to size up the situation. He figured Dawn had likely told her how she felt about Molly's coming even before she arrived. The woman smiled. "There's more than one way to cook a chicken. Just clean out the innards and throw the chicken in the pot. You make dumplings don't you?"

Molly's face brightened. "Yes, yes I do."

By suppertime, Jonas was ready for a good meal and he didn't mind having chicken two nights in a row. There were some folks who'd be pleased to have chicken once a week. He was blessed. He needed to remember that.

It was hard when he sat at the table and realized his son's shirt was streaked with blood and mud. Apparently he'd wrestled with the chicken after he caught it. Dawn's hair looked like it hadn't been combed since yesterday when Birdie had cleaned the children up for Molly's arrival. He tried to keep his eyes averted from the blood spatters and smudges on Molly's apron.

He'd rarely seen his children so unkempt. And he'd certainly never seen Molly with hair loose from her roll and hanging alongside her face. Nor had he seen her brow damp with perspiration.

Think something positive, Jonas.

After the prayer, Molly dished out the chicken and dumplings from the pot on the stove. She set each bowlful on the table. She looked on while Jonas took a big spoonful, blew on it, then poked it into his mouth. "Mmmm." He chewed and swallowed. "Good."

He realized he kept nodding too long. The chicken was fine. The dumplings done and tender. The taste was a little weak. He was trying to figure it out when Dawn offered the information. "The milk's still in the cow."

At least Molly could draw water out of the well.

Molly filled her own bowl and brought it to the table. After one taste, she laid her spoon down and put her hands on her lap. "Oh, I should have used milk instead of water. Can't I do anything right?"

"Well, yes," Jonas said. "You did pull the feathers out of the chicken."

Molly laughed, despite the flush that had

rushed to her cheeks.

Dawn giggled. Jonas felt it was better to laugh than cry. Thinking better of either, he asked, "What are your plans for tomorrow?"

Molly seemed pleased that he asked. "Well, I mentioned to Birdie that I needed to get some plants or seeds for the flower beds out front and she said she would bring some by in the morning, the Lord willing."

"That's one of her favorite phrases," Jonas said. "Never know what might come up to call a preacher or his wife away."

Molly smiled. "Yes, she was just passing by this afternoon on her way to see a woman who recently had a new baby. Birdie told me she has a flower business."

"Birdie's done that as long as I've known her," Jonas said. "She gets many of her plants from the forest and she's ordered some from catalogs. Her business is on her porches and in her gardens. You can trade her a chicken for the plants."

"Oh, I can pay her."

"No, ma'am." He felt he'd said it too shortly. But a man had to take care of his own family. Helping out was one thing. But he couldn't take money from a woman. "I mean, anything that is needed here is my responsibility. I appreciate your help, Molly. But I can't take your money."

"Jonas, I still have a lot to learn in the 'helping out' area. I could at least make things . . ."

She focused on her bowl of thin-souped chicken and dumplings when he shook his head and said, "No, thank you." He regretted the look of defeat on her face and the look of victory on Dawn's. He attempted to ease the tension. "I know our life here can't compare with that in the city. But we have all we need. Dawn's school fees have been taken out of what I made teaching history and mathematics. And I have substituted a few times at the school in the mining camp."

After a sip of sweet tea, she put her hand to her throat. "I didn't know you taught school."

"I'm not the full-time teacher," he hastened to explain. "But there have been times when the cove has been without one; I've helped out. So have the pastor and Birdie. Now I'm called upon for a few special classes or lectures at Pine Hollow School, the one in Coalville, and sometimes down at Poplar Grove."

He suddenly felt like a chicken without its feathers, the way she looked at him. What did she think? That he was just an ignorant country bumpkin? He forced away the thought, realizing he had lumped her into one not-too-savory category of city women.

Changing the subject, he said, "Sometime tomorrow you might think on making sure the children get their baths and seeing their clothes are clean for church on Sunday."

Molly got the point and continued eating her supper. Jonas didn't consider her enough of a relative or friend to allow her to help out with money. Strange, money didn't seem to mean much to Jonas. It had meant everything to Percy.

She would just have to learn what she didn't know about taking care of his house and children. Dawn offered no information.

Caleb willingly helped with anything and everything, but a three-year-old's knowledge was limited.

That morning she'd cooked eggs and pancakes, cleaned up, and breathed a sigh of relief when Birdie had stopped by. She offered to teach Molly how to kill a chicken. That's when Jonas had ridden up and saw the fiasco of the poor chicken with its neck broken.

She'd spent the afternoon wondering where Dawn had run off to and keeping her eye on Caleb. At least he was content to play as long as she was in his sight. She spent a couple of hours fixing supper. It wasn't that she didn't know how to do things. She just didn't know how to do them without modern conveniences like she'd had in the city.

Then she tasted her chicken and dumplings. A feeling of inadequacy struck her. At least she realized what she'd done wrong. She'd used water instead of milk. But, milk came from the cow, and the cow was in the pasture grazing. Was she supposed to take the stool and pail into the pasture?

Before Molly could ask, Caleb picked up his bowl and drank the remaining juice.

"Caleb, the polite thing to do is try to get all the juice with your spoon. Like this."

He picked up his spoon and slurped the air. He and Molly laughed.

With enthusiasm, he laid down his spoon. "Cookie, cookie."

Molly's laughter halted. She had not seen any cookies in the pantry. She hadn't thought to make any. Even if she had thought, there hadn't been time.

"We're all out of cookies," she said. "Tell you what. Let's make cookies in the morning."

"What kind?" Dawn asked, with a challenge in her eyes.

Molly had no idea. "What kind would you like?"

The girl shrugged. "I like muffins."

Besides glistening with dried chicken soup, Caleb's face glowed with a happy smile. "I like everything." He spread his arms wide. "And canny."

Thank the Lord for that. Otherwise she'd be a total failure.

After supper, Dawn said she needed to study her Bible verses.

"Fine," Jonas said. "Right after you gather the eggs."

He turned to Molly. "I'll clean the kitchen."

She protested. "I came here to help, Jonas. You must let me."

"You are, Molly. You haven't stopped since you got here, and you worry about not being able to do anything. If I were in the city, I'd be having trouble adjusting, too. You deserve a break." He spread his hands. "Sit on the porch or take a walk."

"But I have so much to learn."

He nodded. "You will. You only arrived yesterday."

Strange, she felt like she'd been here a very long time.

"And," Jonas said, "there's still your milking lesson tonight."

Molly relented. At least the kitchen was

neat as a pin compared with last evening. She took a cup of coffee to the front porch and sat in a rocking chair to enjoy the cool evening before grappling with that cow.

Caleb played at her feet. The hounds came up, gave her soulful stares, then flopped on their bellies near the steps.

Molly thought about the high hopes she'd had when she arrived here. Now she wondered if she had come here with some mistaken idea of recapturing her own childhood or having her sister's children fill her own need to have children in her life. She did want to help but wondered if she was making more trouble for Jonas by her ignorance of life here. And Dawn wasn't warming up to her.

But Jonas had asked her to come here. If he didn't run her off, she would stay long enough to know if she was a help or a hindrance.

Her thoughts turned to Jonas's teaching history and mathematics. He said he'd taught last year. Did that mean he hadn't since Sarah died? He probably couldn't, having to look after Caleb. Maybe, if she could learn mountain ways, he would ask her to stay on after Dawn's arm healed. But she had a lot to learn. And fast.

A little later, while sitting on the stool and

daring to watch her hands, she determined to point the other way, hoping the milk would then squirt into the bucket instead of on her.

She shouted for joy. "Miracle of miracles! It worked, Jonas."

He grinned, and the cow mooed.

Jonas gestured toward the cow. "She's pleased."

"Hallejulah!" Molly said. "I've learned to please a cow."

Six

On Saturday morning, Jonas arose early, fixed his own breakfast, and was ready to go into the fields by sunup. He didn't want to begin his day with a prayer that God give them wisdom and strength to face the day, then have it followed by a tension-filled meal with Molly and Dawn. And, too, there'd been no rain since last week's downpour. It would come soon, and he'd like to get the plowing done in the far fields on the other side of the creek. Already, bean plants and tomato vines made an impressive sight and the cornstalks were at least six inches high.

Dawn came in, rubbing her eyes just as he gulped down the last of his coffee. "I'm getting an early start, Dawn. Molly should be up shortly to fix your breakfast."

"What about my clothes?"

Since she broke her arm, Jonas had helped her with her clothes that needed to be buttoned. "Molly can help you."

"I don't want her help."

"Then do the best you can, daughter." Turning from the defiance in her eyes and the tremble of her chin, he hastened out the back door.

For several hours he and his horse plowed, stopping only for a few water breaks. Dawn running toward him caught his attention. He wiped his sweat-covered brow with his sleeve. The location of the sun indicated it was midmorning.

His heart leapt with concern that something dire had happened. At least she was fully clothed, so maybe she allowed Molly to help her with the buttons on her dress.

"Pa. Pa."

With a prayer for patience, he waited.

"Miz Birdie brought Preacher Evers with her to visit."

"I'll be there directly." He and the horse both needed a break. A look at the plowed field and the smell of freshly turned rich earth brought a sense of pleasure that this had been a morning well spent. He crossed the creek, washed his hands and face in the cool liquid, and shook off the water.

Clothes hung on the line, swaying in the gentle breeze.

Jonas entered through the back door and

realized everyone had gathered out front. He walked out onto the porch. Caleb was showing the pastor his train.

The women were taking plants from the wagon and laying them near the flower beds. Jonas shook the pastor's hand.

When the women approached, he saw that Molly held a plate covered with a napkin.

"Like I told Molly yesterday," Birdie said, hiking up her skirt a few inches to ascend the three steps to the porch. "Ira had a funeral up in the Black Mountains and needed to visit the sick. Otherwise, he'd have been here sooner."

"I understand," Molly said. "Come inside. We'll need something to go with these cookies. I just brought in the tea pitcher from the creek. It's nice and cold."

"Oh, I remember," Birdie said, following her inside. "You always brought tea for Sarah, didn't you?"

"She loved it."

Jonas wished he'd been more attentive to the things Sarah had loved. Some remarks she'd made had rolled off him like a leaf being carried off down the creek and disappeared.

They all followed Molly into the kitchen and sat at the table. Dawn obeyed when Molly asked her to get glasses from the cabinet. Molly poured tea for each of them. She handed Caleb a cookie, then the others took one.

Pastor Evers did the proper thing of expressing condolence over Molly's loss of her husband and praised her for coming to help Jonas and the children. Jonas watched Dawn's mouth open for a deeper breath, then she looked toward a window as if she'd rather be elsewhere.

That concluded, Birdie's eyes brightened and her tone of voice lifted as it did when she began talking about her upbringing in the city. She met Ira Evers at church when he was attending seminary.

"It's been hard," she said. "I was so much in love it didn't matter at first when he felt called to preach back in this mountain hollow."

Ira set his glass down rather hard. "Well, if it's so hard, why are you still with me, woman?"

Birdie gave him a sassy look. "Well, Ira. I reckon it's because I still love you. You know what the Bible says. It's better to live in an attic with a good man than a mansion with a quarrelsome one."

"I think you got the gender wrong, there, Birdie."

She shrugged. "The meaning's the same,

74

whether it says man or woman."

"Yes," he agreed. "I know exactly what that verse means."

She hit at his forearm. "Why, Ira. You behave yourself now."

Molly laughed with them. Jonas picked up his glass and drank from it. He and Sarah used to insult each other like that. It meant their love was so strong they could joke and laugh. Maybe they did it so they could then say they were just joshing and they'd hold each other and . . .

He shook away the thoughts, determined to listen to the conversation the two women were enjoying, talking about the city.

Miz Evers said that cove life was so demanding, particularly for a preacher's wife who is expected to be available to everyone, she hadn't returned to the city over a dozen times in the past forty years. She leaned toward Molly with an expectant look. "What does the church look like that you attended?"

Caleb listened to anything Molly said. Even Dawn's eyes were riveted on her aunt who told about the big brick church with its stained glass windows that reached from the floor to the high ceiling. There was a pipe organ, a choir loft, carpet down the aisles, and cushions on the seats. There were classrooms for children in Sunday school.

Dawn spoke up. "I thought it was a sin to go to school on Sunday."

"It's not like regular school," Molly said. Dawn sipped from her glass, but Jonas knew she was interested. She liked school. She liked learning.

Molly talked about Sunday school being a place where they talked about the stories in the Bible. In the summertime, when school was out, they even had a week of Bible school. "If you do that here in the cove, I'd love to help."

Birdie became eager. "We could plan something like that. Most of the parents would spare their children for a few mornings."

Molly said, "Oh, I'd love it."

"I didn't think you'd be here that long," Dawn said, reaching for another cookie.

At about the same time, Pastor Evers said, "Are you biting off more than you can chew now, Birdie?"

They all pretended not to hear the impertinence in Dawn's voice.

"Would it hurt to try, Ira?"

"Where would you do it?"

Birdie grinned and gave Molly an "I won" look. "At the school." She turned to Molly. "Church services are held in the school."

She poked Molly's arm. "Oh, that reminds me. Let me tell you about the preacher who was here before Ira. He was a circuit rider. Came through every two weeks or so."

Ira was already chuckling, although he'd probably heard it more times than Jonas had.

Birdie enjoyed being listened to. "This circuit rider would hold church wherever he could. Well, he came to the school. He would bring paper with the words of a hymn written on it. He would read a few lines of a hymn, then the people would sing them. He was reciting 'Amazing Grace' and got to the third verse. He squinted at the paper and said, 'I left my glasses at home and can't see the words.' The people started singing that, then they all burst out laughing."

Molly laughed, not as exuberantly as Birdie, though. Ira amazed him, always laughing at Birdie's stories no matter how many times he heard them. After a hearty chuckle, Ira stood. "Let's give the women-folk time to talk."

"Come on, Caleb," Jonas said. "Let's get a chicken for the pastor. There's extra eggs in the creek, too."

The pastor grinned. "Just what I hoped you'd say."

"We have plenty of canned peaches, Birdie," Molly said. "Let me trade you some for all those flowers."

Birdie slapped a hand to her chest. "Ira's been after me to make him a cobbler. We'd appreciate that. Sarah put up the best peaches."

"Dawn," Jonas called, "you want to come with us?"

"No, sir. I want to go look at the flowers."

He didn't hear Dawn make a reply when Molly said, "Figure out where you want them, Dawn. We'll plant them later."

Jonas told himself the distance between Molly and Dawn wasn't serious enough to talk to the preacher about. Dawn would come around soon.

"Okay, Caleb, let's go chase a big fat hen."

Caleb began a singsong chant. "Big fat hen. Big fat hen."

"You're doing a mighty fine job there, Dawn," Birdie said. "And with only one good hand, too."

"Thank you." Dawn continued moving the plants around.

Molly picked up a potted plant. "This is so unique."

"My trademark," Birdie said proudly. "Being a preacher's wife I have to grow Jack-in-the-pulpits."

Molly marveled at the green curved leaf, making a protective covering for the jack in the center of the plant, resembling someone standing in the pulpit. "It's gorgeous."

"You'll have to come and see the rest of my plants." Birdie climbed into the wagon, set the glass jar of peaches beside her, and took the reins since Pastor Evers was holding on to the protesting chicken for dear life. They all said their good-byes.

Molly turned to comment on the plants Dawn had laid out on the grass. "Is that how you want them in the bed?"

"Mama did it this way."

"I'm glad you remember, Dawn. Your mama's beds looked beautiful. I hope I can do half as well."

"Me, too," the little girl said matter-of-factly. "You'll have to dig that up." She pointed at the weeds.

Molly had planted flowers and vegetables in garden plots, but she'd never dug up beds like these that were about three feet wide and eight or ten feet long on each side of the steps. She hoped her voice sounded braver than she felt. "I'll need . . . a hoe."

Jonas pulled a long green growth, then tossed it aside. "Most of these can be pulled out. I'll get the tools and dig it up." He addressed Molly. "You can rake the weeds out, then the planting can begin."

While Jonas went to get the tools from the barn, Molly took her stained black dress off the clothesline and went inside to change.

When she came out, Jonas approached from around the cabin, pushing a wheelbarrow loaded with a mattock, hoe, rake, and a small shovel. Caleb was examining a plant rather roughly. "Be careful with those, Caleb."

Dawn turned toward him. "Leave them alone," Dawn demanded. His lower lip poked out and he looked at Molly for an ally, but she didn't want to say or do anything to cause Dawn to run off and sit on that hill beyond the pasture where the cow grazed.

"Caleb, while Dawn and I plant these, you can pick up the weeds and these papers and put them in the wheelbarrow."

Dawn carefully removed the newspaper from the root of a fern, not an easy feat with only one hand. Caleb eagerly picked up the paper and proudly deposited it into the wheelbarrow.

Molly told Dawn she could loosen the dirt around the edges of pots with the little hand tool so the blooming flowers would come out easily.

Jonas dug and tossed aside some big roots.

"I know these are ferns." Molly pointed at the small plants that had shiny round leaves. "And these are galax. Those tall yellow ones with dark centers are black-eyed Susans." She shook her head. "I'm not sure of the others."

Dawn named them all. The yellow centered ones with white petals were oxeye daisies. She seemed proud to be sharing her knowledge of wild geraniums, sweet white violets, purple and lavender larkspur, bluebells, and bluets.

Caleb picked up a ball of roots. He began tearing apart the matted root structure. But his getting filthy was better than her and Dawn reprimanding him. Dirt would wash off.

Molly thought maybe she'd made a breakthrough with Dawn as they worked together. Maybe that was the answer. Letting Dawn know that she wasn't here to tell her what to do or try to take her mother's place. They could work together to make life a little easier.

Not until Caleb said, "I'm hungry," did she realize lunchtime had long passed. "One more plant and we can stop."

After planting the last bluet, Molly and Dawn stood back to appraise the work. "Unbelievable," Molly said. "In a few hours

81

we have this colorful, blooming flower bed as if it had been growing for weeks." She smiled. "Dawn, we did well."

Dawn looked pleased.

"You know," Molly said thoughtfully, "maybe we could do something with that old iron pot out back — set it by the back porch and plant flowers in it. What do you think?"

One look at Dawn's face and Molly knew she'd said the wrong thing but couldn't imagine what.

"You can't do that," Dawn said, her eyes pleading.

Molly stared. Then she remembered Jonas said an iron pot rolled back on Dawn's arm, breaking it. "Is it because the pot broke your arm?"

Dawn shook her head.

"Then . . . why . . . ?"

Dawn backed away as if fearful Molly might strike her. "When my arm is healed, I'm going to roll it up that hill. That was a special place for me and my mama. She was going to take the pot up there so we could build a fire in it when the weather was cold. We could be warm, and even cook."

Dawn's words had come fast as if they'd been bottled up inside her for nine months. At least she was talking about her feelings.

That might be good. Molly watched Dawn run around the cabin and knew the girl was going to her and Sarah's special place.

Caleb looked at Molly for a reaction. He never seemed too upset about what took place, just observed. Molly asked for a hug, which he readily gave. How she wished she could envelop Dawn in her arms.

Dawn needed so much more than someone to cook meals, clean the house, and plant flower beds. But each time she thought they were taking a step forward, it seemed they took several backward.

I don't know how to help her.

Other than the undercurrent of tension from Dawn that evening, supper passed without incident. Molly brought a ham from the cellar in the hillside and served it, along with baked potatoes. She'd opened a jar of tomatoes, cooked fresh spinach, made biscuits that were only a little too dark on the bottom. Dessert was a jar of peaches.

At bathtime, Dawn asked Jonas to wash her hair. He refused, saying if she didn't allow Molly to help her, then she would have to go to church dirty.

He knew she hadn't had a tub bath since Birdie helped her on Thursday. "You know you can't get the sling and splint wet," he warned.

With a towel, Jonas took hold of the hot water tank that heated on the side of the cookstove and poured it into the tub in the corner behind the stove for Caleb's bath. He added buckets of cold water and refilled the stove tank. Jonas sat in a chair to watch. He'd warned Molly that the boy liked to duck under the water and hold his breath.

Molly washed his hair with her shampoo that conjured up memories for Jonas.

Caleb went under to rinse his hair and came up so forcefully his hands went down and splashed water on Molly. They both laughed, although she gently chided him. Jonas reveled in the aroma. Dawn came up and stood beside him. Her voice sounded as wistful as he felt. "That smells like Mama. Like — like roses."

After Caleb was clean as a whistle and dressed in a nightshirt, Jonas stood. "We can tuck him in while water heats for Dawn. Then I'll say good night. I'm sure you'll want to bathe."

Molly agreed. "Oh, yes. I don't remember ever being so dirty in my life. After I bathe, I can go to the bedroom and you can take your bath."

"No, it will be way too late by the time more water heats."

"You aren't . . . going to bathe?"

"There's a place out there in the creek where clean spring water cascades down the rocks. Great place for bathing."

She rubbed her arms. "Gives me the chilblains to think about it."

"Me, too," he said. "So I'm not going to think. Just plunge right in. Anyway, the water here's not going to heat up for quite a while."

He didn't need to be thinking of Molly, letting her hair down and bathing in the tub. He missed the times he'd wash Sarah's back and she his. He would rinse Sarah's hair for her. Most times her hair smelled like lavender soap. Sometimes she used the special shampoo Molly brought from the city — that smelled like roses.

Jonas left the cabin for the night. He wanted to get his dousing in a waist-deep part of the creek before dark. He'd been in and out of that creek for much of his life. Cold water was a way of life much of the time in these mountains. One got used to that.

Was he ever going to get used to being without Sarah?

SEVEN

Molly and the children smelled like roses.

Jonas wondered if he smelled like mountain trout. At least that would be better than wearing the odor of a barn that hadn't been shoveled out.

Dawn's brown hair, pulled back from her face and plaited in a fancy braid with a ribbon on the end, looked better than it had since Sarah died.

So far, Caleb's hair was still in place, parted on the side and swept up in a wave over his forehead. Jonas didn't expect that to last long. "You wearing new clothes, son?"

"New clothes," he repeated, patting the waistband of the navy blue short pants, held up by suspenders over a white short-sleeved shirt.

"You look mighty fine."

Caleb nodded, smiling broadly. Apparently, he'd been told that already.

"He's about to outgrow his other clothes," Molly said, as if she needed to explain why he was wearing the outfit she brought from the city.

Jonas felt remiss. "I've noticed that on Sunday, then it skips my mind during the week." Molly had mentioned that she brought clothes for both children, but Dawn was wearing one of her usual Sunday dresses. "Your hair is pretty that way, Dawn," he said, and she smiled. He doubted she could braid her own hair like that, even with two good hands.

Dawn studied him. "Pa, you're dressed up more than usual."

"Not really, Dawn. It's only a tie."

"You don't always wear a tie."

Surely Molly wouldn't think he wore a tie for her. But in a way, he did. He'd seen her fancy clothes before and knew she wouldn't be wearing that now-atrocious black dress that was a reminder of death. In fact, he'd rarely seen a person look so alive.

He mustn't stare.

She came right out and said, "Maybe that's what cold creek water does to a person. Makes him act different. You do look nice, Jonas. Almost like a city fellow."

Whether that was a compliment, he wasn't sure, but he said, "Thank you."

He'd never commented to Molly on her looks or attire when she visited, so he felt any compliments now might not be fitting. He greeted her with a brief nod. What could he say anyway? That she was going to be the talk of the cove in that purple dress with white frills in front and a cameo brooch at the high neck, and a purple hat with a cluster of multicolored flowers on one side. Her honey-colored hair was rolled into a neat, thick roll at the nape of her neck. A few curly strands hung down in front of her ears.

She rode the three miles in the buggy without raising her parasol, but after he held out his hand as a courtesy when she alighted from the wagon at the school, she raised the parasol. He soon realized any compliment he might have paid would surely mean nothing compared to what she received in the churchyard.

Birdie exclaimed loudly that she was the prettiest thing she'd ever seen, just a walking angel, and called others over to meet her. Many had seen her at the funeral, but that had been somber.

Women welcomed her. Men tried to keep their eyes off her and children stared, wide-eyed and with their mouths open. They whispered to each other and stared more.

She smiled, said thank you, and that she was glad to meet them on a happier occasion. He heard Bessie Camron tell her she was sorry to hear that her husband died.

"I'm just trying to make the best of it," Molly said.

"That's all we can do," Bessie said. "I know. I lost my Jim a few years back in one of them mine accidents. I moved away from the camp. Just couldn't stand it no more. So I can see why you'd want to come here. A change of pace is what we need sometimes."

Molly agreed. Pastor Evers rang the bell. Women and children moved together as a family and went inside.

Jonas was aware of the difference in having Molly sit with him and the children as a family. During the past nine months he'd felt lonely in church without Sarah. His wasn't like other families anymore. He felt different, like half of him was missing.

Caleb sat between him and Molly. Dawn sat on the other side of Jonas. Caleb kept looking at Molly while she sang. His son had accepted Molly. Jonas wished Dawn had taken to her. He could raise his son to be a man. But he couldn't give his daughter the woman's touch she needed.

When they stood to sing, he couldn't. His

throat hadn't been able to handle the words after Sarah died. He listened to the words and tried to make them part of his beliefs, like rejoicing when they all got to heaven.

Men and women wore their finest to church. Women who had them wore hats. But Molly dressed nicer than them all.

He remembered when Molly visited and brought a city dress that Sarah had worn to church and had been so pleased. Had Sarah envied Molly? Is that why she had made him promise to let Molly help if anything happened to her? He'd never doubted Sarah's love but now wondered if she'd liked to have had a different way of life. Was she like Birdie, who indicated she preferred the city, but stayed in the cove because she loved Ira?

The pastor's sermon was about having faith the size of a grain of mustard seed and you could move a mountain.

He read that scripture, and Jonas didn't hear much else after the pastor asked, "What's the mountain in your life?"

Jonas began thinking about his mountains. He knew a mustard seed was a tiny thing.

He reckoned his faith wasn't as big as he'd supposed before Sarah died. When things were going well, one could think he had a lot of faith and loved the Lord.

When you lose someone like Sarah you know you shouldn't but you question why the Lord let it happen. He knew better and if it was a test of his faith, he reckoned he failed.

Mountains were all around him all his life. The only moving ones he knew about were landslides and mine cave-ins.

Contrition for such adverse thoughts brought him to a deeper level. He knew mountains that really needed moving were the burdens of life, and that required a spiritual remedy along with one's own efforts.

What were the mountains in his life? There were the ones that required his work such as plowing, planting, tending and harvesting crops while caring for a family. But that was workable. He didn't worry that his children wouldn't have what they needed.

His mountains had to do with acceptance of Sarah's death in a way that brought peace. Finding a way to help his daughter adjust to a life without her mom.

How was faith going to work those things out?

He'd always thought his faith was sufficient. But it had never been tested like this.

When they stood for the final song, Jonas

wished he'd listened more carefully. Maybe the pastor had said something that would help. How could he get that faith? He'd always known — when he had Sarah.

What had his faith been in?

God?

Or Sarah?

There were no stained-glass windows. Open shutters allowed the smell of fresh pine, rich earth, and fragrant flowers to waft in on the cool breeze.

The singing wasn't like in the city church where everyone sang the right notes and all together. Here, each one had his own rhythm and sang from the heart. The voices weren't trained, but they sang to the Lord. The setting took Molly back to her childhood and made her happy. She sang out, too, louder than she would have in the city. There, she had to blend. Here, one could sing as they wished and not worry about holding a note too long or singing too loudly.

Before the preacher started preaching, he introduced Molly to the congregation, although she'd met some of them in the yard. He said she was Sarah's sister who had come to help the family. He made a point of saying that Jonas was happy about that, even if he did have to sleep with the animals in the barn.

He also told that she was trained in piano and voice and maybe would honor them with a song some fine Sunday.

After church the people were kind and complimentary, but Molly felt she didn't really fit in. She wondered if she should not have worn her fine clothes. But she didn't have any other kind.

Wearing a plain skirt and shirtwaist would be hypocrisy since she would not feel right in church without her finest. And clothes shouldn't matter. Some of these people were nicely dressed, like Jonas, Birdie, and Pastor Evers for instance. A few men wore overalls; and a few women wore scarves instead of hats. She did not think less of them, so they should not think less of her.

Molly told herself it didn't matter. But joy leapt into her heart when a couple of women approached her and said they met her at Sarah's funeral. One was BethAnn Mason who lived near Birdie. Her husband worked at a store in town.

Earlene Haynes lived a couple miles up the mountains from there and her husband worked as a clerk in the miners' commissary in Coalville.

The two women were direct opposite in

looks. BethAnn was pretty, blonder than Molly, fair and petite, while Earlene was several inches taller than Molly, had a wholesome look, and hair dark as a raven's wing.

They each had children, a reminder to Molly that they were no older than she, but she was childless. Caleb and William, Beth-Ann's young son, sat nearby playing with twigs and making train sounds. Molly surmised that Caleb had told William about his new train.

Dawn stood several feet from Jonas, talking to a girl about her age. When Molly looked, they both turned their faces away. Molly suspected Dawn would be telling the girl about her.

She concentrated on BethAnn and Earlene, however. Both apologized for not being able to help Jonas more.

"Sarah was our friend," BethAnn said, her eyes becoming moist as she glanced at Earlene, who nodded. "We feel so bad," she said, speaking for them both. "We've offered to make up a schedule for different ones of us to watch the children if he'd bring them to our cabins."

"But you know men," Earlene put in. "They're so proud and not about to be beholden."

BethAnn's bare hands caught hold of Molly's gloved ones. "We're so glad you came to help Jonas."

"Is there anything we can do to help?" Earlene asked. "Tom wouldn't mind my coming there with a woman in the house. Otherwise, he thinks it wouldn't look fitting."

BethAnn was nodding. "We really want to help."

Molly related some of her mishaps in trying to conquer that cooking stove and the cow.

They laughed and Molly joined in. "It wasn't funny when Jonas and the children had to eat burnt chicken."

Earlene shooed away any concern with a movement of her hand. "I declare, hon, we can help you get the hang of any ol' woodstove. Anyway, Sarah got one of those newfangled ones. Jonas managed to have it brought in last year on the Coalville train, then brought down the mountain in a wagon. It's not often that the coal train brings anything from the city. But Jonas got it."

Molly wondered how he managed that. "Oh, you two are so kind —"

BethAnn groaned and her fair face reddened. "Not really." She sent a sly glance toward Earlene who grimaced. "We were whispering in church —"

"As if that wasn't bad enough," Earlene said and rolled her eyes much like Dawn had a habit of doing.

BethAnn nodded. "We wondered what we could do to make ourselves an outfit like you're wearing. Oh, not exactly the same, but grand like that."

"I didn't make this."

BethAnn waved her hand. "We didn't think so. But I have a treadle machine and the store down in Poplar Grove where Tom works gets in some mighty fine bolts of cloth. Earlene and I trade off things. We both know how to use that machine."

Earlene was nodding. "If we could look at some of your outfits, we could come up with ideas that look . . ." She searched for a word.

"Citified?" Molly grinned, feeling a closeness to these two women.

Both women nodded, returning her grin.

Molly stuck out her gloved hand. "A deal."

BethAnn's expression looked like a child's with her favorite candy. "What day should we come?"

Molly had no idea. Before she could answer, Birdie joined them. "I have a bone to pick with you, Molly," she said. "Oh, you girls stay. It's something anybody can hear."

EIGHT

That night, instead of going outside after supper, Molly washed Caleb and dressed him in his nightshirt. Afterward, Jonas said, "What's your Bible verse, Caleb?"

His eyes widened and his chest poked out with his deep breath. He looked at Molly when he answered, "Jesus swept."

Jonas chuckled and said, "Very good."

Molly laughed and hugged Caleb. "Oh, you precious boy."

His little face lit up like a candle on a Christmas tree, having pleased her.

"Okay, buddy. Time for bed."

"I'm not Buddy." His lip came out, and his eyebrows drooped. "I'm Caleb."

"Bedtime anyway."

Molly felt such joy at Caleb's every word and action. Even when he was displeased or tired, there was so much wonder in the child.

Each night since she'd arrived, Jonas had

suggested she take a break and walk outside while he did the dishes, then put Caleb to bed. She couldn't imagine that Sarah would ever do such a thing. And didn't Jonas ask her here to do the things Sarah had done? But she wasn't really close family. Maybe bedtime was too intimate to include her. At least he had let her get the boy ready for bed.

As if reading her mind, Caleb reached for Molly's hand. "Mama come, too." Jonas must have detected the hope in her eyes. He nodded.

Jonas got on his knees beside the bed, so Molly knelt on the other side of Caleb who placed his little hands beneath his chin, bowed his head, and began thanking God, then got into "God bless" everyone and everything he could think of.

Molly marveled at the love in the faces of father and son as they hugged tightly. She couldn't imagine more beautiful words than "I love you, son" followed by "I wuv you, Papa."

Caleb lifted his arms for her, and Molly eagerly embraced him, conscious of the warm little body and tousled hair that still bore the faint aroma of her shampoo. Caleb had his own sweet little-boy smell.

Caleb didn't want to let go, and Molly felt

she would love to cuddle up with him on her lap. In that hug was a world of love where troubles tended to vanish.

Jonas insisted Caleb let go.

Molly looked over at Jonas. "Do he and Dawn hug?"

A troubled look clouded Jonas's face. "They haven't in a while."

Molly had the feeling that "while" was since she'd arrived.

"I don't know if I should force such," he said.

"Could it hurt?"

The way Jonas looked at her with such tenderness in his eyes touched her heart. Softly, he said, "Thank you."

Those two little words, said so sincerely, seemed to say he thought she might be of some value here after all. He went to the doorway. "Dawn, come tell your brother good night."

Molly stood aside, hoping Dawn would concentrate only on her brother. Dawn came stiffly into the room, reminding Molly of the years in the city when she'd felt stiff but went through the motions of doing the expected things, learning to say the right words, and pretending all was well. She hadn't thought anyone cared that things weren't right.

Maybe they, like she now, just didn't know what to do to make it all right.

Molly breathed a prayer. *Oh, Father, please help Dawn revel in the love her little brother so freely gives.* She watched Dawn's face soften in the embrace. Molly barely heard Dawn whisper, "I love you," after Caleb said the words to her. Her eyes closed, and her chin trembled. Someday, somehow, that dam inside her would have to burst. She needed love so much.

Could she ever accept it from her aunt Molly?

The thought staggered Molly.

Did I accept it from Aunt Mae?

As soon as Dawn backed away, Caleb said, "Mowwy sing muh-bwee."

Molly's glance at Jonas revealed neither of them knew what he was saying. Was he trying to say "Molly" instead of "Mama"? She didn't remember how she thought when she was barely into her third year of life but felt it could be confusing for a young child to hear a woman called by her name and "Mama." She understood the "Mowwy" but not the "muh-bwee."

Jonas's glance questioned Dawn, who shrugged and took on that defiant lift of her chin. She turned, saying, "I'm going to my place," as she left the room. Molly knew she meant the hill beyond the pasture.

Jonas tucked Caleb in. Molly sat on the side of the bed, gently stroked his forehead with her fingertips, and sang one of the hymns she'd sung in church. Soon, his smile relaxed and his eyelids drooped.

Molly walked into the kitchen where Jonas stood looking out the window, toward the hilltop that Dawn said was her place. He faced Molly when she said, "I love that little boy so."

"I know." His brow furrowed. "He's transferred the love he had for his mama to you."

"I keep telling him —"

Jonas's raised hand halted her words. "I'm not condemning you. I'm just concerned about his heart being broken again."

So was Molly. Caleb's heart and her own. She sat on the bench. "Maybe it's true, Jonas, that it's better to have loved and lost than not to have loved at all."

"Maybe?" He stepped over to the table. "Surely you can answer that."

Molly turned away quickly from his questioning stare. She looked away and headed for the cabinet door and opened it, hoping it would hide the flush she felt on her face. She thought of her love for several people, particularly Sarah. In spite of the hurt that loss brought, she was glad they had renewed their relationship and loved each other, however briefly. "Of course I know." She set the cup down a little too hard. "Would you like coffee? I . . . need to talk with you about something."

He pulled out a chair and sat at the table.

Molly poured the coffee and set the cups on the table, then sat opposite him.

She didn't know how he would react to what Birdie asked of her after church. Since she was here to help with the children, she needed his permission. She plunged right in. "Birdie asked if I would go with her to the mining camp school. She said the missionaries are coming this Wednesday."

Jonas nodded. "They come every two weeks if the weather is good."

"That's what she said. And she goes in case they can't be there. She said you could explain about the Bible verses."

After taking a swallow of coffee, he set the cup down. "Missionaries come from Virginia every two weeks, weather permitting. They make their rounds of the schools where there are no churches and teach Bible verses to children of all grades. Birdie does that at Pine Hollow School. The children recite their verses and get prizes. When they recite 250 verses by memory, they win a Bible.

Fewer verses get them a book, a toy, or candy."

Molly huffed. "How can a child remember 250 verses?"

"Not so hard. The Twenty-third Psalm has six verses. I'm sure you must have learned that at an early age."

Molly nodded. "Oh, and the one about making a joyful noise unto the Lord. I had a teacher who sang it."

He brightened. "Dawn was trying for the Bible, but she . . . lost interest awhile back." He looked down at his cup.

"If I can remember, I can sing it while I . . ." She stopped and laughed. "While I burn dinner."

Jonas's cheek dimpled. Would that man never laugh? "If I sing it, I'll bet both Dawn and Caleb could learn it."

Jonas agreed. "Likely."

"And the Beatitudes," she said.

He added, "The Lord's Prayer."

Molly lifted both hands above her head. "And the Ten Commandments. Well, of course they can learn 250 verses. One a day or a whole psalm in a week."

Jonas looked almost happy. "And they don't have to recite all 250 at one time. They recite what they've learned during the two weeks."

Molly was so excited. "And you know, Jonas, it wouldn't hurt me to brush up on what I learned years ago. If I'm going to teach a . . ." She stopped at seeing his surprised look. Then she remembered — like Dawn said, she wasn't going to be here that long.

That must be why Jonas suddenly looked puzzled.

"Never mind," she said. "I'm getting way ahead of myself. Is it all right if I take the children to the mining school on Wednesday? Birdie said she might even turn that job in Coalville over to me every two weeks."

"I think that would be a wonderful thing, Molly. Dawn became acquainted with some of the children there when she and Sarah sometimes went with Birdie. Dawn was afraid she would forget her verses before Birdie had time to listen at Pine Hollow."

"Oh, thank you," she said. He rose from the chair. When she said, "Another thing," he sat again. "BethAnn and Earlene want us to exchange visits. Is that all right?" She didn't care to reveal their reasons. That might sound like foolishness to him.

"Good," he said. "It's good you're making acquaintances. Being a part of the community."

"Yes, I would love to have friends. Oh,

but I won't neglect the children. Both women have children, and BethAnn has a boy Caleb's age."

"Yes, I know. They used to visit." He took a deep breath. "Anything else?"

"Well, just one. Is there a pencil and paper around? I'd like to make a few notes."

"There's some in the bedroom closet, in a box." He stood. "I'll get it."

He returned with a box and rummaged through it. "These are some of my papers that I use in teaching the history class. Some of Dawn's school papers are in here, too. Someday she may want to see what a good student she was."

He found a pad of paper and a pencil then returned the box to the bedroom. She got up to pour herself a cup of coffee. "Would you like another cup?" she asked when he returned.

"I'll pour myself another cup and take it to the lean-to. It's almost dark, so I may have to yell for Dawn to come home."

Molly walked to the window and saw the young girl walking toward the cabin, her head bowed. She kicked a small stone. "She's coming."

Upon leaving, Dawn had run from the cabin, across the pasture, and up the hill. When returning, she meandered.

"Jonas," Molly said thoughtfully, "how do you have enough faith to move a mountain?"

She wondered if he thought she'd asked a foolish question. He didn't answer readily. Finally, he said, "That's something I want to study on tonight."

Jonas thought on it. The brightness of Molly's eyes. Her resemblance to Sarah, yet so different. Sitting at the table, talking over things was like what he and Sarah used to do. Sarah's talents were taking care of the home, wanting many children. She had finished high school but wouldn't have considered teaching, other than teaching the children at home. She'd helped Dawn with Bible verses when she'd first started learning them.

But he needed to think on Molly's question. It involved belief in Jesus as God's Son who died for the sins of mankind, who was resurrected and lives. Faith was believing God's spirit dwelt within those who believed. It involved repentance, obedience, hope.

He'd thought he had it. But now that God hadn't let life go the way he wanted, how much faith did he really have?

He turned to the concordance of his Bible. Faith. He read that faith was the substance of things hoped for, the evidence of things not seen.

How could he return to a childlike faith?

He couldn't. He needed an adult faith, based on the Word of God, not earthly circumstances. He'd believed God gave Sarah to him, and his children. He was supposed to believe God had a purpose and plan in all that He did.

Lord, I've not given my hurt and anger to You. I've seen men and women change their way of life when they come to You. I've seen healings beyond what a doctor can do. I haven't blamed You when I've known of a man thrown from his horse and he died out in the woods before anybody could get to him. I didn't blame You when there was that mud slide and the Hankins' cabin went down the side of the mountain. I didn't blame You for that barn burning. Or when Jeb got drunk and shot a man over a horse deal that wasn't fair. Not even when my pa died in the mine accident. But I've blamed You that Sarah and our little baby died.

Your Word says we live in a fallen world. One in which Satan rules. But You're always with us. You don't give us more than we can bear. How Molly can be an answer to our family's needs, I don't know. I don't understand. And I've fought that from the time

Sarah asked for it.

A lot of that was based on my dislike of Mr. Pierpont and knowing how some city folks look down on some people just because we prefer life in the mountains. Lord, I don't always understand Your ways. But I know You have a plan and purpose for those of us who believe in You and try to live right. Help me accept what You bring my way. And if I make mistakes in my decisions, like bringing Molly here, work it out for us. Give me understanding to know what to do and what to say.

NINE

The next morning, Jonas still wondered. Where was the line between keeping one's distance and acceptance? He might try conversation, like he and Molly had last night. Since Dawn wasn't offering any help, he might try that instead of running off to plow by daybreak.

Molly came in from the creek with eggs for pancakes when Dawn rushed up to the kitchen door, all excited. "Pa, baby chickens have hatched. I counted eight."

Caleb got up from the kitchen floor where he was playing with rocks representing coal he would haul in his choo-choo train. "Chickies," he said, heading for the back door.

"Just a minute, son. That hen might flog you if you get too close to her little ones. Here, let me take you." Jonas picked him up. Before he could ask if Molly wanted to go, she dropped the big spoon into the bowl and rushed to the door, excitement all over her face.

Dawn opened the door of the chicken house. The hen and little ones went out into the wire pen. Molly gushed. "Oh, look at those adorable fuzzy little balls peeping like that. Aren't they beautiful, Caleb?"

He began saying he wanted a chickie. He wiggled, and Jonas put him down. Upon seeing Caleb approach, the hen squawked and spread her wings. The little ones ran underneath. The hen's wings came down and covered them protectively. She sat as she had on the eggs before they hatched.

Caleb kept pulling on his papa's pants, saying he wanted to hold a chickie.

"The mama hen doesn't trust us yet. We'll just walk on by. When she sees we're not going to hurt them or take her babies away, I can pick one up and let you hold it."

"Oh, I want to hold one," Molly said, looking as eager as Caleb.

"Have you never seen baby chickens before?" he asked in wonderment.

"Oh, yes. My aunt and uncle took me to fairs and I've held them. They're so soft and sweet. But, Jonas, how did this happen? I mean, every evening Dawn brings in the eggs for you to take to the creek. How do you know which ones have yolks in them and which ones have chickens?"

Jonas had tried so hard not to laugh at her. But this one started low in his belly, rolled around, reached his throat, and there was no controlling it. If one must laugh, it might as well be a big one. He'd had only shallow laughs for such a long time, this one felt odd in his stomach, like pulling a muscle.

The way Molly lifted her chin, tolerating his laughter, made him laugh even more. He looked at Dawn who had her hand over her mouth, and her shoulders were shaking.

"Sorry." He issued a couple more quick sounds still left inside him. "That just struck me so funny."

"Good," she said saucily. "It's about time you laughed, even if you have to make fun of me to do it." She hurried over to Caleb who was trying to open the door to the henhouse. She helped him.

The rooster went out, strutting like a proud papa.

They all went in. "I don't mean to make fun, Molly."

"Laughter's good, Jonas. I've wanted to laugh and cry about my ineptness. I mean, if it's funny, it's funny. Why run around all solemn with a mule's face?"

Was that how he looked to her?

But she wasn't looking at him just now. Her gaze swept around the chicken house as she tried to avoid the droppings on the floor and looked up at those roosting. "So that's where they lay their eggs."

"Sure is," Jonas said while Caleb ran around chasing chickens and Dawn stepped inside. "Each one usually lays one a day."

She looked around, puzzled. "Where are all the roosters?"

"He went outside when you opened the door."

"You have only one?"

"That's all we need."

"Well . . ." She looked around again, and finally spoke in a low tone. "There are a lot of chickens in here. Doesn't he get — you know — tired?"

Jonas felt it coming again. Why try? He laughed heartily. He wiped the moisture from his eyes. The Good Book said there was a time to weep and a time to laugh. He felt like doing both. Weeping because he hadn't laughed in so long. Somehow it felt like a release, as if he'd like to follow it with weeping. Like there were things stuck deep inside him that needed to be let loose.

"I'm sorry. It's not that funny."

She stood with her hands on her hips, but he got the impression she enjoyed seeing him laugh. He supposed that was better than the mule's face. She shrugged. "I'd like to see you in the city trying to use a telephone."

He leaned back, pretending to be insulted. "Beg your pardon, ma'am. I know about city ways. I did go to university." He grimaced. "But to be honest, the first time I talked into a telephone, I yelled as if trying to force my voice into the next county. Believe me, the laughter of my peers was torture to a young mountain man trying to fit in."

"Well, when you're finished, I'd like to know about the poor rooster. How often do you have to get a new one?"

He emitted a few spurts of laughter between explaining. "A hen doesn't have to have a rooster around to lay an egg. She does it all on her own."

He knew she didn't believe him. "Then why have a rooster?"

He lifted a finger. "Ah. The rooster is only needed to fertilize an egg. That's where the baby chickens come from."

"Well," she said, "get ready to laugh again because that brings this discussion back to my first question. How do you know which eggs are fertilized?"

"I don't," he said. "But the hen does."

She looked skeptical.

He explained. "I don't know how the hens know, but they do. They make a nest for themselves, lay the fertilized eggs in it, and sit on them to keep them warm until they hatch."

"Isn't that amazing?"

He'd taken such things for granted as far back as he could remember. For an instant, however, he was seeing this through her eyes. "Yes," he said, "I suppose it is amazing."

"So, if I gather eggs, I would take the ones which a hen is not sitting on?"

"Yes and no. I let the hens sit on the fertilized eggs so we can have new chickens in the spring to grow up and lay more eggs, and of course grow them for trading and eating. Little chickens might not survive the winter, so we can take even the fertilized eggs then."

"Okay," she said. "You can tell me when you have enough new chickens, then I can gather the other eggs."

"I think you're beginning to understand."

She smiled, and he smiled back.

It's all right, he told himself. *She's my wife's sister.* He turned toward the doorway. "My stomach is yelling for some of those eggs and pancakes."

The tension had lessened for Jonas. If his daughter was ever going to accept Molly, he needed to set the example. He had no business avoiding her when all she wanted to do was help.

He stuck around the kitchen and even turned the pancakes. "Just helping," he said.

"Oh," Molly said in her sassy way, "are you trying to say you're tired of that charred flavor?"

"It really hasn't been so bad."

"I will learn," she said.

That was a lot like Sarah. When she put her mind to something, she did it. "I'm sure you will."

While they ate, Dawn gave Caleb a verbal lesson on how to handle baby chickens. She would take him out after he ate. That resulted in his having to be warned not to poke an entire pancake into his mouth.

"You two can water the flowers, too, after you see the chickens," Molly said. "Now, Caleb, you mind Dawn."

Instead of rushing off to work, Jonas started clearing the table and putting the dirty dishes in the dishpan. "I think I've been remiss not to help you more, Molly. I'm sorry. You've had to find your way around, and Dawn hasn't been any help. I haven't really known how to approach this and didn't think it right to say you have to do things a certain way."

"It's all right, Jonas. We've all been feeling our way through."

"Is there anything I can do or you need me to explain to you?"

Molly laughed lightly. "I'm glad you asked." She tilted her head to the side. "You can tell me how to cook, clean, raise children, feed a pig, and get an egg from a chicken."

He began nodding. "I get your point."

She cleared away some of the dishes. "But like I told you last night, I have help coming this week and I'll learn all those things. Like you've said, it takes time."

"In the meantime, I can help a little more around here. Believe it or not, I did help Sarah."

"I know," she said. "She told me."

That was remarkable.

A silence hung between them for a moment. He saw the look of sadness cross her face that matched the sudden sinking feeling he had in the pit of his stomach, talking about Sarah in the past tense.

"Jonas, I never had to cut wood, kill a chicken, or handle a woodstove. After marrying Percy, I planned parties, volunteered at the hospital, told others what to do. I did some needlework. I continued with voice and piano lessons. After a while, I began taking in piano students."

Something tightened in Jonas's stomach. A few days ago he didn't want Molly here. Now he wondered if she decided the tension was too great between her and Dawn. That she needed to leave.

But for a few minutes, she had taken his mind off his loss. She made him laugh. Caleb loved her. Dawn needed her even though she didn't know it. Sarah's friends took to Molly. Birdie liked her. He should get to know Molly. She was his Sarah's sister.

With an elbow on the table, he placed his forehead in his hand. "I'm sorry I couldn't tell you how Sarah managed the household chores, took care of the children, or got meals on the table at the right time."

"I know," she said. "I'd like your opinion of something. I'll be right back."

"Would you like more coffee?"

He poured the coffee. She returned with a piece of paper, so he sat.

"I made a schedule for the work to be done."

He stared. She wasn't talking about leaving. She was planning how to do more.

He looked at the schedule.

Wash clothes on Monday.

Iron on Tuesday.

Mend on Wednesday.

Sweep on Thursday.

Scrub on Friday.

Bake bread on Saturday.

Church on Sunday.

When he was silent for a moment, she asked tentatively, "Any . . . suggestions?"

"Just one that might make things easier. Sarah used to cook the big meal at noon, and leave leftovers on the table. We could come in and grab a biscuit or corn bread anytime, and have a light supper. That way the house wasn't so hot with the fire going all day."

She exhaled like a weight had just been lifted. "Oh, I like that. Cooking is not my long suit."

She tapped the schedule. "Of course those aren't the only things I will do. But that sort of organizes things. I'll listen to the children say their Bible verses on Wednesdays." He detected the uncertainty in her voice. "And I don't need to wash all the clothes this coming Monday since I did that Saturday morning. I can plan the Bible school when Birdie comes by today."

Jonas could see her interest lay not in housework, but in teaching. He complimented her on the schedule. "Well, one doesn't have to stick to a schedule avidly. I plan to plow but sometimes rain prevents it, so I change plans."

Her schedule looked good on paper. He told her so. "Sounds like a good idea."

"I can't really take the credit. It comes from a song." She began to hum the song.

Jonas knew it.

Her pretty blue eyes gazed at him tenderly. He smiled. He thought her face was more tanned than when she'd come a few days ago. Maybe that's what made her hair seem lighter and her eyes a clearer blue.

Realizing he must be staring, he took a last gulp of coffee and stood.

Dawn and Caleb came into the kitchen.

Jonas looked at his son. "Caleb, let's gather these ham bones for Lad and Lassie."

Molly's eyes questioned.

"The dogs," he said. "They're . . . twins."

He liked to hear her laugh. Now that laughter had returned to his household, he rather yearned for it.

TEN

Almost all day on Monday, Molly and the children dug potatoes, pulled onions, and picked the biggest squash to put in the cellar for seeds and for supper.

Molly heard an, "Ohhh," from Caleb.

He was holding a little green tomato. When they all looked, he tried to put it back on the vine. Molly held back any laughter since his little face clouded like he was about to cry. He'd been told not to pick little green ones.

"I just touched it," he said.

Molly nodded. "Sometimes they just fall off. But that looks like a really fine one for lunch." She smiled and he brightened, then put it in the basket with the other vegetables.

Dawn hadn't made any adverse remarks all day, and by evening Molly doubted anyone had the energy for negativism.

They all went to bed a little earlier than

usual, and Molly felt she hadn't slept so soundly since arriving in Pine Hollow. She did recall hearing a steady rain during the night that had been soothing.

She tried to rid herself of that groggy feeling with a cup of coffee while looking out the kitchen window, thinking she'd wake up by going to the creek for breakfast food. Then she saw Jonas, with bent head covered by a wide-brimmed hat, sloshing his way up to the house.

He opened the back door, shook the water from his hat over the porch, took off his jacket, and hung them on a peg. She had to smile at the pleasure on his wet face as he held out a basket. "Breakfast," he said.

She laughed. "You must have known I had in mind to feed you biscuits only."

"Crossed my mind," he said and smiled.

He poured himself a cup of coffee while she made breakfast. He walked over to the table and looked at her sheet of paper.

"Ironing day," she said. "I'm glad the weather cooperated Saturday and dried all those clothes."

Jonas looked up. "I'll take the children to the barn. You probably need a break." Just as she opened her mouth to protest, he added, "Sarah used to say for me to take the children out and give her a breather.

Especially on ironing day."

Molly appreciated his thoughtfulness. As soon as she began ironing, she was particularly grateful not to have Caleb underfoot when she needed to move the handle from one iron to the other on the stove.

As time passed, she relished the hours alone, thinking, absorbing her surroundings. She'd been so busy, so tense, so concerned about caring properly for the children, then having Dawn's resentment, Jonas's distance, and Caleb's possessiveness.

She could understand Sarah's needing a break. Sarah would have done many chores that Molly hadn't yet learned. Besides that, she had pregnancies and miscarriages. No, Molly knew she had no room for complaints.

As the day dragged on, she began to miss them. A loneliness settled around her. She'd come here, determined to immerse herself into this family's life and help ease the pain of losing Sarah.

Things hadn't happened quite as she wanted or expected. She'd come to know this family in so many ways. You couldn't live with people, sleep in their bed, have responsibility of their home, touch their animals, watch their chickens being born, or bring their milk with your own hands without becoming absorbed into that family.

She'd observed a man pine for his wife, struggle with his faith, care about his daughter's withdrawal, try to carry on in spite of all that, plow his fields, mend his fences, care for his cattle, encourage her, eating burnt food without complaining — seeming to think some of her ineptness was not a matter of ridicule but amusement — and ultimately easing tension by laughing. He kept hoping that he, she, or time would make a difference in the way they all felt about their loss. He was trying to go on with his life, even leaving his home and living in the same building as his animals in hopes of accomplishing something.

She supposed he was rather . . . remarkable.

He'd begun to mention that she did things like Sarah had. They both had been concerned about Caleb's attachment because he needed his mama so much. Was Jonas in danger of the same kind of attachment?

She thought of how long it takes to really get to know a person. When Percy worked as bookkeeper for her uncle, she would pass his office and see him working on books, sometimes even late at night.

After Uncle Bob brought his new bookkeeper, Percival Pierpont, to dinner, Molly thought she knew something about him. After that, he took her to restaurants for dinner, to the fair, to a horse race. During the three months they associated with each other, she supposed she spent the equivalent of forty-eight hours with him, including the couple of times he managed to sit with them in church.

Three months had seemed long enough to know a person. After all, her uncle had known him for several months before inviting him to dinner at their home. But when you count the hours, they were fewer.

Here, spending all the hours of the day with a family was getting to know them, not eating out, having fun at a fair, rooting for a horse, or sitting in church. No, getting to know a person wasn't what one observed in public, but what went on in their everyday lives.

She'd learned that the hard way.

She'd learned more about Jonas and his family in a few days than she had about Percy in a few months.

Around noon, when she called them in to eat the meal she'd had time to concentrate on, Jonas commented that it was quite tasty. She'd prepared mountain trout that swam into the trap Jonas rigged up in the creek.

She'd baked bread, made a sweet potato pie, and fixed fresh spinach from the garden.

Dawn even made the comment, "It's not burnt."

Molly took that as a compliment and felt quite pleased with herself. "I discovered that less heat and more time makes for a better meal." Her pleasure turned to chagrin. "Oh, I don't mean that I need to be alone. Oh, my, no. I missed all of you today. I . . . oh, dear."

Jonas chuckled. "Around cooking time is when Sarah shooed us all out of the kitchen. That's one reason she wanted the partition separating these two rooms — to get us out from under her feet. Cooking and keeping a little one away from the stove's not easy. Believe me, I know. Especially during the winter months when we have the stove and fireplace going at the same time."

Molly looked at the fish on her plate. Good for her. She'd managed to remind him of Sarah again. Would someone ever like her for herself?

The rain let up for a while, and from the kitchen window Molly watched Jonas, Dawn, and Caleb shovel straw and waste into a wheelbarrow. Jonas rolled it to the newer compost pile near the older one that was fertilizer for the gardens and fields.

The rain had cooled the air somewhat, but she felt hot and sticky from the day of cooking and ironing. Dark clouds rolled in again and a downpour began. It looked to her like one that would fall hard and vanish quickly.

A little later, upon hearing laughter, she peered out the kitchen window again. With a gasp of surprise she ran to her room to grab her rose shampoo and several towels. She dropped the towels near the back door then rushed across the porch and down the steps. Not only would she get a bath, but she wouldn't have to scrub her shirtwaist and skirt as hard on wash day. With a squeal of delight at the deluge, she joined her temporary family, exclaiming, "I've gotten wet plenty of times but never had a rain bath before!"

"Not as cold as the creek," Jonas said.

She'd never bathed outside or fully clothed. But it was delightful. They all splashed around, washed their hair, lifted their faces and drank the rain. Laughter was the outstanding quality of the hour. Molly gave permission for Caleb and Dawn to make Lad and Lassie smell like roses.

After drying off on the thirsty towels, they changed and, having worked up an appetite, had a supper of their choice from beneath the tablecloth, which included freshly baked oatmeal-raisin cookies.

Jonas had smiled upon looking at the table covered with the cloth. "That's what Sarah used to do."

Jonas said the children couldn't go back outside and get into the mud. "You two can read or play games. How about checkers?"

Caleb shook his head. "Meow."

Even Dawn joined them in the front room. Molly listened to Jonas's explanation of "Poor Tom," although she remembered having played it years ago with Sarah and other children.

Caleb was first to be the cat. He got on all fours and meowed. First Dawn, then Jonas, patted him on the head and said "Poor Tom" three times without laughing. When he came to Molly, she'd already felt the laughter bubbling up at his antics of a cat chasing a rat. She laughed at him.

Dawn's acting like a cat getting milk squirted into its mouth was hilarious, particularly when she shook her head so vigorously her hair covered her face. Then it was Jonas's turn. The sun had lightened his hair that looked golden-brown against the darker roots. She quickly repeated "Poor Tom" three times and he moved on.

When she patted his head, she wasn't even thinking about his catlike antics. She'd never before touched his hair. Jonas was the only one who could make no one laugh which meant he was the loser unless Molly made no one laugh.

Molly didn't expect Dawn to laugh at her and wondered if she'd even pat her head and say "Poor Tom" at the appropriate time. Before Molly could get on all fours, they were already in hysterics when her knees got caught in her dress. Dawn couldn't hold back her giggles when Molly had trouble moving from one person to the other on all fours. She didn't think her restrictive movements were catlike but had no doubt she looked funny — ridiculous, really.

Molly had not felt so happy and pleased since she arrived. She was being accepted.

She hoped Dawn might start a conversation after supper while the two of them cleaned up the kitchen. She felt as though she'd accomplished something today, put a good meal on the table, and was beginning to know how it felt to be part of a close, loving family.

She could even imagine having a man like Jonas for a husband, a loving child like Caleb who kept every moment filled with joy, energy and challenge, and even a daughter

128

like Dawn who would be fine . . . with time.

She lifted her face from the dishpan and looked beyond the window. She could almost see the corn growing. The gardens, pasture, fields, and hills looked fresh and clean after the rain. The bean fields glistened with silver droplets.

A good feeling of contentment welled up inside. Absently, she began to hum a tune from a faraway memory.

A plate crashed to the floor. Molly jerked around. The look on Dawn's face was as broken as the pieces of china scattered on the hardwood floor.

Dawn's chin quivered and her eyes sparked with misery. "Don't you dare hum that tune! That's my mama's song." She turned and ran into her room, slamming the door.

Jonas came from the front room. "What happened?"

"An — an accident."

Molly was thinking a more apt question might not be "What happened?" but "Why had it happened?"

She thought she knew. But she needed to be sure. If she was right, then she knew what Caleb had wanted her to sing last night, and why. Dawn had known, too.

Jonas's eyes were troubled. "We've all

broken dishes or something, but it's never been a big issue. Every little thing upsets her now." He opened the pantry door and got the broom. "Were you talking about anything in particular?"

Talking. "No. We weren't talking at all."

"Maybe with time this will straighten out. Anymore, I just don't . . . understand." He began to sweep the broken pieces into a pile.

Molly thought she did understand.

Dawn's life and heart were as broken as that plate lying shattered on the floor. The plate would be thrown into the trash. What would happen to Dawn's brokenness?

Molly sighed. "If only I could find a way to get her to talk about her feelings."

He straightened and held on to the broom. "Today was good, kind of like how things used to be. Sarah loved playing games. I think Dawn enjoyed today."

Molly turned and gazed out the window and looked toward the clearing sky.

Yes, today had been good. But far from ideal.

Jonas liked her better when she did things like Sarah.

But Dawn resented her more when she did things like Sarah.

She lifted her eyes toward the sky where several dark clouds lingered.

Lord, I don't know a lot about faith.
But I'm learning a lot about mountains.

ELEVEN

"Oh, my." Molly looked out the window early Wednesday morning upon hearing a wagon pull into the back. "I didn't expect Birdie this early." She hadn't finished breakfast.

Jonas opened the back door before Birdie had a chance to knock. Instead of the pleasant expression Molly expected, Birdie's face was flushed. "There's been an accident." She set a large basket on a clean section of the kitchen table.

While all eyes were set on her, she clasped her hands in front of her ample chest, then spread them, making motions as she spoke rapidly. "A rider came to the cabin early this morning to get Ira. The missionaries were on their way up here when one of the wheels came off and the carriage turned over. Mr. Simpson is just bruised, but Miz Simpson is in the hospital in town. She's unconscious. I just stopped by on my way down there."

After stopping long enough to take a deep breath, she brushed at the gray streak in her hair. "Molly, I was so looking forward to taking you up to Coalville." She pointed to the basket. "Besides food, I have my Bible and records of what the children recited last week. Is there any way you could let them know what has happened?" Her dark eyes pleaded. "Could you listen to their verses?"

Molly had thought of a dozen reasons why she wanted to go to Coalville and take part in Birdie's project. Now, more than a dozen reasons loomed large in her mind why she couldn't. She glanced around at Dawn and Caleb. "I have the children, and I don't know how to get there."

"I thought of that." The flip of Birdie's wrist implied Molly's protests were futile. "Extra food is in the basket. And there's only one main road up to Coalville." She pointed at Jonas. "He can give you directions."

Molly sent Jonas a pleading look, hoping he would agree that she couldn't possibly go alone.

Instead, he nodded. "I'm sure Molly will help you out, Birdie. Don't you worry."

Birdie clasped her hands and looked toward heaven, then grasped Molly's hands.

"Oh, Molly, you're an answer to prayer. Thank you, dear. I'll return the favor somehow. Just you wait and see."

Before Molly could protest, Birdie was out the door and gone.

A long moment passed before she could face Jonas, trying to control her frustration. "Jonas, I can't do that."

"I know," he said. "I'll take you."

She had to take in a deep breath. "You know?" Her hands went to her hips. "You think I can't handle a horse and wagon?"

His eyebrows lifted. "Can you?"

"No, Jonas. I'm planning to drive into every mud hole so the wheels will fall off, we'll turn over, and all go to the hospital."

He lifted a hand. "Sorry."

Caleb looked from one to the other, wide-eyed. Molly glanced at the boy and apologized. "I was joking, Caleb." She addressed Jonas. "Sorry."

After a deep breath, she explained. "My uncle let me try my hand at it when we'd go to the market. I don't care for riding in those newfangled automobiles. They're smelly and break down all the time. I prefer to pass them up with a horse and buggy any day. Besides —" her voice rose with conviction — "I can even walk faster than those contraptions."

"That's something you won't have to worry about in these parts." Jonas got up to pour himself another cup of coffee. He lifted the pot with a questioning look, she nodded, and he refilled her cup. "From what I've seen of automobiles, they couldn't make it up these mountains." He put the pot back on the stove. "Hasn't been long since trains have been able to come up this far."

Oh dear, now she'd convinced him she could handle a horse and wagon. But she hadn't driven one in the mountains. How could she handle a horse, keep a young girl from running off, and control an energetic little boy who might decide to jump out and chase a squirrel or something? She didn't want to say that maybe mountain women could do anything, but she was a city girl. She'd been trying so hard to be a mountain woman.

She hurried over to her cup of black coffee.

Jonas must have read her mind. "Like I said, Molly, I'll take you."

"The rain has stopped. What about the planting?"

He grinned. "Well, if you can take time out from your schedule, I suppose I could break my routine."

"You pick a most inconvenient time for humor, Jonas."

That little-boyish look appeared on his face. "I'm really being conniving. If I take all of you up the mountain, then on a planting day, each of you can help plant."

"I would be glad to help plant, Jonas, anytime you need me."

He nodded. "I know that. But no matter how experienced you might become, I'd never approve of you and the children going up to Coalville alone."

Dawn spoke up. "Pa, I've been studying. Could I say my verses there?"

"Dawn, for a long time now you've been saying your verses at Pine Hollow."

Molly jumped in immediately. "Wait a minute. If I'm to be in charge today, then I make the rules." She watched his face carefully, not wanting to overstep. A gleam of approval was in his eyes. "So, I think anyone who wants to say their verses may do so."

Dawn scooted off her chair. "I'll change my clothes."

That was the most enthusiasm Molly had seen in Dawn. Maybe something good would come from this after all.

After they headed up the mountain in the wagon, sloshing through some puddles but mainly rolling along on the hard-packed road, there wasn't much Molly could do but listen.

She turned in the seat to keep her eye on Caleb and to glimpse Dawn's expression. When they got in the wagon, Caleb had wanted to sit up front but she told him to sit right behind her. He could reach up and touch her at any time. Dawn sat right behind her papa.

"Jonas, I wonder if you would do me a favor if we have time."

"If I can."

Molly decided her conversation should be for Dawn's benefit even if she had to say things Jonas already knew. "You know Sarah and I lived in the mining camp when we were children."

He nodded.

"One of my fondest memories is a big mulberry tree near a creek up there. I wasn't much older than Caleb, and I guess Sarah was close to Dawn's age. Our mama would take us down to the creek."

Molly turned her head further back. "Dawn, you said that song I was humming last night was your mama's song. It was your grandmother's song before that. Mama would take me and Sarah down to the creek and we'd sing and dance around that mulberry tree. There was one bush in the front

137

yard at our house. We would dance and sing with other children in the mining camp and pretend that bush was the mulberry tree."

Dawn's head turned toward her. "My mama did that with us."

Molly's heart skipped a beat. Dawn's tone of voice did not sound resentful, but reminiscent.

Jonas smiled. "Sarah even had me doing it."

Caleb laughed. "Muh-bwee."

"Yes," Molly breathed. "The mulberry bush. I guess we could call that song an heirloom."

After a short silence, Dawn asked, "What's an heirloom?"

Dawn was actually conversing with her. "It's something that's passed down from one family member to another, like a piece of jewelry, or a man's watch, a special book, a painting, or even a lacy handkerchief."

"Mama had her mama's ring. Pa said I can have that and Mama's rings when I grow up. I guess that's an heirloom."

"That's about the most special kind."

After a thoughtful moment, Dawn looked at her. "You and Mama had the same mama, right?"

"Yes, your mama and I are sisters. Just like you and Caleb are sister and brother.

You have the same mama."

"What heirloom do you have from your mama?"

Molly was about to say she didn't get anything. But there was one thing. "Well, Sarah was the oldest, so she was entitled to the ring. When Papa sent me away with my aunt and uncle, he gave me Mama's Bible. And it has some of her favorite recipes in it."

Dawn's glance met Molly's. "Can you cook them?"

Molly didn't know if that remark and the little gleam in Dawn's eyes meant she was being sarcastic, trying to joke, or just conversing. At the moment, it didn't matter. She felt that overwhelming sense of loss that she felt when all she had of her family was her mother's Bible and a few recipes. "No. I never tried."

"But I guess you read your mama's Bible."

"No." Molly felt the roles had been reversed. She felt like a grieving child and didn't want to be questioned about things so private — that still hurt. "But I keep it with me."

A solemnity settled on Molly as they neared the place where she spent her early childhood. The air was cooler the higher they went. She drew her shawl closer around her shoulders. The craggy peaks jutted straight up into the sky in some places. In others, she could look down on beautiful hollows where horses and cows grazed. There were small farms with fields of corn. Others appeared to be beans, some tobacco, all lush and green, likely having been nourished by frequent mountain rains.

For a moment she closed her eyes against an unwanted memory of another small farm. Forcing herself to think of other things, she thumbed through the papers, along with a list of instructions that Birdie had left with her. She began to read.

After a while, she looked around. "I keep hearing that same sound, like a bird is following us."

"It's not a bird," Caleb said. "It's a chickie."

Caleb lifted the corner of the tablecloth covering the basket. He took out a little peeping chicken.

"Oh, Jonas. Caleb brought his pet with him."

Jonas looked around and laughed. "Be easy with that baby chick, and I don't want you crawling all over the back of the wagon while we're going up the mountain. Dawn, you watch him."

"I already told him what he has to do,"

Dawn said. She took a few seeds from her dress pocket and laid them on her lap. "Now put the chickie in my hand."

Caleb passed the chicken to her hand. Dawn told him to pick up the seeds. He held them in the palm of his hand and they giggled as the chick pecked at them.

Caleb giggled. "It tickles."

After a while Dawn told him to put the chick back in the basket because it was just a baby and needed to rest. Caleb obeyed, then picked up one of the books Molly had brought with them.

Molly had wanted to come home. Now, here she was, in Coalville. The houses looked the same. She, Sarah, and their papa had lived in a box house like these that had only two rooms. That was after the fire.

As they rode through the mining camp, Molly said, "I . . . think that's the one we —" Her voice broke. "— we lived in."

Jonas glanced at her. "What's wrong, Molly?"

She swiped at a tear. "I didn't know this would be so emotional. The memories are just flooding in. Coalville is where I spent the happiest and saddest days of my life."

Twelve

Jonas understood what Molly must mean. During his courtship of Sarah, she confided in him how the loss of her mama in a fire had been so heard to bear. She didn't go into detail, and he didn't press her for information. Her early life had been like Molly's. But like Molly, Sarah had seemed happy and outgoing.

He admired Molly's way of not wallowing in self-pity but turning her attention to other projects.

Jonas realized she wasn't as blasé as he'd thought at first. Her hurts went deep. She just put on a happy face, while his was — mulish. He'd have to do better.

He did, later, while standing around the wall of the long, one-room schoolhouse with other men and women. The male teacher expressed sympathy for the events of the morning, which prevented the missionaries and Birdie from coming, but welcomed

Molly as the teacher who would listen to their verses.

If he didn't know her, he might not notice that lift of her chin, which meant, not stubbornness as he had once supposed, but determination in the face of whatever challenge presented itself. He could admire that.

She took a moment to gaze around the room, smiling, trying to put the nervous pupils at ease. He knew they didn't often see a lady dressed so finely in pale yellow and wearing a multicolored shawl. Yet, her outfit was plain compared with her frilly, fancy ones. She had been astute enough to dress down in a nice, but simple, skirt and shirtwaist.

Two older girls near the back whispered. Jonas heard one say, "She's purty."

The other spoke in an awe-filled voice. "She must be a queen."

When Molly smiled and spoke, however, she sounded more like a loving encourager. He wasn't sure Birdie would be as accommodating as Molly who said she wouldn't count off if they missed a word or two, as long as it was close and the meaning clear. She gave an example. It would be fine if one turned words around like "For God so loved the world" to "God loved the world so much."

"Now," she said, "we will start with the younger ones first. But, before I call on the first graders, my nephew would like to say his verses. Caleb McLean."

Caleb left his place on the front row and toddled up to Molly. He faced the other children.

He took a deep breath and looked over at Molly. She smiled. "Caleb has two verses. Go ahead."

He kept looking at her. "God is love."

"Perfect," she said. "Now, the other one."

His overload of confidence came quickly. He faced the front, leaned forward slightly, and spoke loudly and distinctly. "Jesus swept . . . the fwoor."

Molly gave a cue by beginning the applause to cover the giggles and one boy's hearty spontaneous laugh. Adults were laughing, too.

Why Caleb decided to nod as if bowing, Jonas had no idea. Maybe it just came natural, like his penchant for attention.

Jonas motioned and Caleb ran up the aisle to him, like he'd been instructed.

Molly cleared her throat as the applause died down. "Any additions like that are not acceptable, unless you're a three-year-old."

Tension vanished as the children realized Molly wasn't going to bite them and a mistake wouldn't be disastrous.

Using the alphabetical list Birdie had left, Molly called Billy Adams.

The boy raised his hand. "I don't have one."

"That's fine," she said. "Ellie Brooks."

Caleb leaned next to Jonas's ear and whispered loudly. "I wanna say my verses again."

The two girls at the back looked around. One giggled and the other put her hand over her mouth. Caleb was entertaining, but this was not the occasion. Jonas took him outside where an older woman watched small children sitting on a blanket beneath a tree, waiting their turn to be pushed on a swing.

"I can watch this one if you have other children to recite," the woman said.

He thanked her. "I would like to hear my daughter recite in a little while. She's an M, so it will be awhile."

One little boy got up and started to walk away. To the boy's delight, Jonas scooped him up and held him high. Then he set him back on the blanket. Wanting more, the boy started to get up again. "Hold on," Jonas said. "If you're real nice about waiting your turn and mind this nice lady, after my daughter says her verses, I have a surprise for you."

Caleb clapped his hands. "Surprise. Surprise."

"Now don't you be guessing, Caleb. This is to be a surprise for everyone." Jonas put his finger to his own lip.

A light began to dawn in Caleb's eyes and he put his finger to his lips, lest the secret spill out. He pulled on the woman's skirt. "I said my verses."

"Oh," she said, taking a little girl out of the swing. "My, you're a smart little boy."

Jonas urged. "What do you say, Caleb?"

Caleb looked up at the woman with his big blue eyes and said, "Yes, ma'am."

When Caleb's turn came to swing, Jonas hurried back to the school. A boy returned to his seat, amid applause, then Molly called on Becky Hill. There were two *J*s who recited, one *K,* and then Dawn.

She didn't look at Molly, who gazed at her fondly, but kept her head down until she turned and lifted her chin in that way characteristic of Sarah and Molly. She began, " 'To every thing there is a season. . . .' "

Sarah would have been proud to see her little girl, looking so ladylike in a school dress and her hair brushed neatly to her shoulders. Her arm being in a sling didn't detract from her appearance at all.

Jonas had been blessed with bright children. He couldn't bear the thought of Dawn spending her growing-up years taking care of him, the way Sarah had with her pa.

He didn't think she missed a word in all those verses. Neither did she, apparently, from the pleased look on her face when the children and adults applauded.

Jonas returned to the yard and took the warm little chicken from the picnic basket. None of the little ones got bored after that and when the others were dismissed, adults and children alike enjoyed the running, pecking, and peeping of the little chick that seemed to like attention as much as Caleb.

The teacher, wearing a grin, came up and stood by Jonas. "Thank you for the entertainment." He laughed lightly. "For your boy and the chicken."

Jonas glanced toward the school. "I trust all went well with the recitations."

"Perfect," the teacher said. "I like the way Miz Pierpont had applause after each child recited. That hasn't been done before, but I could see it helped everyone, particularly those who forgot their words and had to start over. I realized they need to be applauded for effort."

Jonas agreed.

The teacher grasped Jonas's arm. "Like I

told Miz Pierpont, we'd be real proud to have her come and teach a special class like you've done with history and mathematics. Being from the city, and having graduated college, she could likely teach a lot of subjects."

Jonas grimaced. "Not too many, though. I need the job."

The two laughed lightly. But Jonas knew that a lot of teachers as educated as Molly didn't want to take a job back in these mountains. They'd want a city job.

Finally, when Jonas felt the chick could take no more, he scooped it up and returned it to the basket. Dawn and Caleb climbed into the back of the wagon.

At Molly's request Jonas drove out to the miners' camp where two-room box houses sat in rows on dirt yards. Obviously, life was meager. That wasn't what Molly mentioned. Instead she spoke of fond memories. "Sarah and I were so close in those days. She tried to be like a mama to me after . . ." She swallowed hard. "After Mama died."

"Nobody can be a mama except a mama," Dawn said.

"I know. And we hear that good comes from everything. Losing our mama may be what helped her be such a wonderful mama to you and Caleb."

Jonas heard the sadness in Molly's voice and glimpsed the starkness on her face. He longed to do something to help, particularly since Dawn was implying that Molly's efforts in their home were in vain.

"You're right about one thing, Dawn," he said. "We can have only one natural mother. But many people fill the role of parents. In some ways, my own grandfather was more like a papa to me than my own. I loved him as much."

"It's not the same," Dawn pouted.

Caleb reached around and caught Molly's sleeve and said, "Mama."

How long, Jonas wondered, could he or Molly overlook Dawn's remarks? He hardly knew which ones he should attempt to debate, or ignore, or agree with. He took his cue from Molly who changed the subject. "Dawn, you said all eight verses of chapter three of Ecclesiastes," she said, "and I'm so proud of you."

Jonas also complimented his daughter, who then began to talk about others who recited.

Following Molly's direction, Jonas drove to a spot where the mulberry tree stood majestically. "There it is!" she exclaimed, as excited as the children had been about the chick.

Her enthusiasm seemed catching. Even Dawn was in reasonably good spirits. "You can take the chick out," Jonas said. "But don't make him run or play. He must be very tired after all that activity at the school."

Forcing any contemplations aside, Jonas felt rejuvenated. This outing reminded him of when he and Sarah took the children and enjoyed a ride, a visit to neighbors, or a picnic.

He helped Molly spread the cloth out on the grass and set out the lunch Birdie had prepared and Molly had added to that morning. In a clearing by a creek beneath craggy peaks reaching into the sky, how could anything not taste good? Birdie must have assumed he would accompany Molly and the children. The basket held fried chicken, biscuits, cheese, strawberries, cookies, and a container of water, complete with four glasses.

He realized what he'd been missing by not having taken the children on outings when the weather had begun to warm up.

After well into their eating, and watching the chick peck around in the grass, Molly pointed to the tree. "That's a mulberry tree, Caleb. The very one your mama ran around when she was almost Dawn's age."

Caleb's eyes widened and he began saying, "Muh-bwee," over and over in a singsong voice.

Jonas said, "He remembers. I was afraid he'd forgotten everything about her."

"We can teach him not to forget," Molly said. "It's good to remember . . . the good times."

Jonas was beginning to realize that remembering and talking about the good times eased the pain of loss.

When Caleb finished eating, he took Molly's hand, singing over and over, "Muh-bwee."

Molly laughed. "We have to go around it. You two going to join us?"

Dawn shook her head. Jonas decided he'd best just watch. "You two go on and play while Dawn and I do all the cleaning up."

He and Dawn put everything back into the basket, then sat in the grass watching. Molly and Caleb couldn't reach each other's hands around the tree. Molly took one of his hands and they danced around it with Molly singing and Caleb doing his best to join in.

Even Dawn laughed when they stopped to make the motions of washing their hands and their clothes. Dawn said, "If he ever washed clothes like that he'd drown himself."

Molly ran around the tree, hid, then peeked out at Caleb with a playful, "Boo." Her hair was coming out of its roll and she finally took the pins out and shook it free with her hands.

Her long blond hair, which reminded him of corn silk, hung down like Sarah's had. It was naturally straight but had the wave of having been in a roll. When she stood still, it hung almost to her waist. It reminded him of times when he'd run his fingers through Sarah's wheat-colored hair. Yesterday, when wet, Molly's had looked more like Sarah's.

He missed his wife, but it was different now — less painful.

"Pa, you look like you went away." Dawn's words brought his eyes around to her.

He exhaled heavily and picked up a blade of grass. "I was thinking about corn and wheat."

"Like you said this morning, Pa. We can help you plant. I only plant with one hand anyway."

He chuckled and drew her close for a moment. "Okay, daughter, you get the chick and I'll get the basket. We need to head back down the mountain."

She looked up at him. "It was a good day, wasn't it, Pa?"

He smiled. "Yes. Better than staying home and planting."

She nodded.

He wondered. Were some mountains beginning to move?

THIRTEEN

"Wait and see!"

That's what Jonas had heard Birdie say on Wednesday when she needed to go down to Poplar Grove.

Not much time had passed. Early Thursday morning Birdie rode up and joined them for a cup of coffee at the breakfast table. She announced that the missionaries wouldn't be able to continue their journey into the Black Mountains.

"The mister will be fine. His bruises will heal," Birdie reported. "The missus has a concussion and must remain in the hospital for a while, then they need to go back to Virginia and take it easy. So, I'll be going further into the Black Mountains since they can't." She peered over her cup at Molly then set it down. "How did things go at Coalville?"

"Nobody complained," Molly replied.

Jonas saw the pleasure in her eyes and the

slight color in her cheeks. Modesty became her.

He couldn't let it pass with that. "She's a natural teacher. Believe me, I've seen plenty of them."

Birdie folded her hands beneath her chin and smiled with a triumphant look in her eyes.

"Parents and children alike responded well." He laughed and told about Caleb reciting his verses.

Birdie laughed, spread her hands, then clapped them once. "I knew all would go well. Just by the way you have come to these mountains in a time of need speaks well for your love of children."

"Oh, I do," Molly said. "Those children in Coalville stole my heart. They were so eager to show what they'd learned."

Birdie shook her finger at Molly. "Yes, and for days I've been thinking and praying about your ideas for a Bible school. The Lord won't let me forget. Didn't I hear BethAnn and Earlene say they're coming here today?"

"Yes," Molly said. "So I thought the children and I would help Jonas in the fields, then I can visit with them this afternoon."

That was the end of Birdie's "wait."

Next came "seeing" from Birdie Evers' organizational point of view. She planned out the days for Molly, with Molly's eager anticipation and offered her own suggestions.

Dawn began clearing the table, one dish at a time, and even enlisted Caleb to help her.

"My," Birdie said, "you're a helpful child and with only one good hand, too."

"I can do my part," Dawn said. "And it won't be long 'til I can use both hands."

Birdie smiled. She looked down at her cup and picked it up. Jonas knew Birdie realized Dawn was clearing the table to prove she was useful and they wouldn't need Molly much longer.

Not need her?

That thought lingered in his mind.

The Lord knew what Jonas needed and brought Molly here to teach him that.

He needed to see activity in his house again. After Sarah died, some of the men had come to offer help. Their womenfolk would bring a pie or a casserole but that stopped after a while. And a wife couldn't go to a man's house and take care of his children when there was no woman in the house. He only asked Birdie at emergency times. She had a full life visiting the people in the cove, helping with their needs, having missionaries and circuit riders stay in their home when needed, taking care of her plants and her own household, and doing her volunteer work at Coalville and Pine Hollow schools.

He could understand why Molly seemed like a godsend to her.

Jonas took Caleb to the barn with him. The chickens were glad to get the seeds but clucked and scattered at Caleb's chasing the little chicks. After Dawn watered the plants in the flower bed, she joined him in the barn. She headed toward the ladder leading to the loft.

"Dawn," he called. She stopped and held on to the ladder. He had to try to find out what was in her mind. "Molly is becoming a big help to us and the community. You can see that, can't you?"

He didn't know his little girl's expressions anymore. What kind of emotion moistened her eyes? Was it anger, hurt, frustration?

She took a deep breath and lifted her chin. "Pa, she looks a lot like Mama. She has a pretty voice like Mama, though it's different. She loves Caleb kind of like Mama did. She likes to help people like Mama did. But, Pa, she's not Mama. She shouldn't be in our house."

"Where do you think she should be?"

She answered immediately. "In the city." Her frail shoulders rose with her rapid breaths. "I see you look at her sometimes the way you used to look at Mama. Are you thinking of letting her take Mama's place?"

I look at her like — what did that mean? How did he look? And when? Was Dawn making that up? Had Dawn sensed his longing for a woman of his own, the memory of his wife? It wasn't Molly he looked at. It was memory.

Wasn't it?

He tried to dismiss Dawn's remark. After all, she was only a nine-year-old girl. What did such a young child know about looks? He'd been nine once upon a time. He thought back to what he knew. He knew when his parents were angry, when they were sad, playful, loving, disappointed, worried. Yes, he knew those things as far back as he could remember, without his parents saying a word.

He would have to be careful of his thoughts about Sarah when he looked Molly's way.

"No," he said finally. "You've said it yourself, Dawn. Nobody can replace your mama."

Dawn blinked, heaved another sigh, then

hastened up the ladder and disappeared into the loft.

The day would come when Dawn's arm would be healed. Then they could go back to being the way they were before.

Is that what Dawn wanted?

Would she be happier?

Caleb would be sadder.

And Jonas . . .

How could he answer the questions in his mind, when he wouldn't even allow them to form?

Molly's change of life for the better really began on Thursday. Birdie brought Earlene, BethAnn, and her son, William. A teenage girl named Rhoda came to watch the little boys and brought her sister Nettie who was a friend of Dawn's.

The young girls joined the women when they struck off for the blackberry bushes and wild strawberry fields. Rhoda was helping the little boys build a train station. Jonas said he'd be within shouting range in case Rhoda needed him.

When they returned midmorning, Molly learned how these mountain women canned their fruit for the winter season. Molly brought out the empty jars she had washed after using their contents for a meal. Other jars were stored in the cellar. The other women had their jars in Birdie's wagon.

They put big rocks in a circle, built a fire in the center, put a big washtub over the fire, and poured water into it. After filling the jars with berries and sugar, they tightened the lids and boiled the jars for twenty minutes.

While the jars were cooling on the back porch, the women made pies with the fresh berries they hadn't canned.

"I've never seen days go so fast," Molly said the following day when they picked beans while the pot of water was heating.

"We'll save the biggest and best for Jonas to keep for planting next spring," Birdie instructed.

They filled twenty-four glass jars with green beans, water, and a half teaspoon of salt in each jar for seasoning.

After they put the lids on, Birdie clapped her hands. "Now, we let those boil for four hours."

"Four hours?" Molly could hardly believe they needed to cook so long.

Birdie explained. "It takes a while to cook in those jars. And, too, the heat kills the bacteria, makes pressure, and as the jars cool they are vacuum sealed." She spread her hands. "Then when you open them this winter, you'll have green beans as fresh as they've been picked today."

"I love it when we work together like this," BethAnn said. "Now, let's dig some potatoes and then we'll spread out a great lunch."

Birdie agreed. "Ira said he'd come by if he could."

Earlene laid her hand on Molly's arm and smiled. "We women used to work together like this with Sarah, too."

Molly was so glad to be included with these mountain women working together. She'd never had such close fellowship with women like this. When married to Percy, she maintained an appearance but never got to know them personally. These women talked about their husbands, children, and daily living. They cared about each other, and Molly wanted to be that kind of person.

During the next days and weeks, the group of women went to each other's homes, picked berries, green beans, and sugar peas and shelled peas. Each day, they would divide up the jars and each woman took her portion home to put in her cellar or pantry.

Sometimes the men got together and helped plow, plant, pick, and eat.

Molly realized this activity could go on all summer and there would be other produce toward the end of the season. Tomatoes were coming on, and she began to fix fried green tomatoes for their big meal. Soon, she'd be canning red, ripe tomatoes.

One afternoon, after the men had helped each other in the fields and they all ate together, the women were cleaning up while jars cooled.

"Tomorrow," Birdie said, "is candy-making time."

Molly learned that children could appear not to be listening and prove you wrong. From several feet away the two little boys looked their way. Caleb clapped his hands like Birdie had a habit of doing. "I want canny."

Birdie ducked her head and gave him a long look. "Tomorrow."

"Tomowwow," he repeated and sighed. Will stuck out his lip.

BethAnn laughed. "Those boys act like tomorrow is forever."

Molly wiped her forehead with her sleeve. "Although I love this activity, I sometimes think all this work lasts forever."

Birdie lifted a finger. "You're right. Making sure there's enough to eat here in the mountains is a never-ending job. You'll be grateful for this when winter comes and you're holed up in that cabin."

Molly felt a jolt. "I won't be here this winter."

Birdie gave her a long look then patted Molly's shoulder in a sympathetic gesture. She must have sensed that Molly would like to be here. Then she gestured toward the peas being shelled so they could can those. "We have to get most of this done before the Fourth," Birdie said.

"The fourth what?" Molly asked.

The other women laughed. "Oh, our big Fourth of July festival."

When "tomorrow" came, they gathered at Birdie's house, first admiring the gardens of beautiful plants and flowers imaginable and unimaginable. Her front and back porches were full, also.

Birdie proudly talked about them all. "I don't believe in weeds," Birdie said. Their eyes followed the gesture of her hand toward a field of wildflowers that she had tamed into rows. "They're all God's creation," she said. "You just need to put them in the right location. He did leave some things for us humans to do."

They laughed and agreed. Soon, on Birdie's long wooden table, she laid out the ingredients for peanut butter roll ups. She mixed powdered sugar, butter, and vanilla flavoring in a large bowl and kneaded it.

"What's that festival you mentioned?" Molly asked.

"The Fourth is the biggest event of the year. We celebrate, dance, play music, sing, play games, and eat."

Earlene laughed. "And this is one time we try to outdo all the others." She stared at Birdie's hands, now patting her mixture out on waxed paper. "Birdie always wins blue ribbons with her plants."

Birdie lifted a white sugared hand. "That's because I'm the only one in the area who has a flower business."

"Yes," BethAnn put in, "but there are others who bring plants. Anyway," she said, looking at Molly as she continued, "people all over the mountains come and we compete with everything from pigs to pies."

"Including Earlene's prize-winning peanut butter." Birdie scooped peanut butter out of a jar with a big spoon and spread it over the mixture she'd flattened on the table. "And right after the festival might be the best time to hold our Bible school."

Molly watched Birdie powder her hands with the sugar, then begin to roll up her handiwork.

As soon as Birdie cut the roll into half-inch slices, Molly delighted in the little white wheels with alternating spirals of white and brown inside. Earlene and Beth-Ann reached for a piece. Birdie laughed and stuck one into her mouth, so Molly did the same.

"Hmmm. Deli-thuth," Molly mumbled with peanut butter sticking to the roof of her mouth.

Despite the pleasant sweetness dissolving on her tongue, the wonder of these new friends, and excitement over the festival and Bible school, her mind went a step further.

Dawn's arm should be healed by mid-July.

Where would she be?

What would she do?

FOURTEEN

Molly hardly had time to think about what she was doing. Her life was a jumble of activity that she dearly loved. There wasn't a moment's spare time, except for that last cup of coffee at the end of day before Jonas left the cabin and went to the barn. As the days grew warmer the drink often became tea or lemonade.

Now, she stood in the kitchen where she and Jonas had just come through the back door. It suddenly occurred to her that she had never been alone with Jonas — anywhere except that initial ride up the mountain. The children, or someone, had always been near. Now, the house seemed . . . different. Quiet — except for her heartbeat in her ears.

Dawn's visit with her friend had been planned during the week. After church, BethAnn asked if Caleb could come home with the family for the afternoon. Tom promised to take William fishing and invited Caleb.

When Molly asked Jonas, he got a thoughtful look in his eyes, then a little gleam she didn't understand appeared and he said, "Yes, he certainly may."

They were all standing together, getting ready to put the boys in their wagon. Tom apologized. "Jonas, I should have asked if you want to come along. We'll be fishing up toward my parents' place and probably have supper with them. BethAnn wants to be alone today to do some women's work."

Women's work. Well, Molly figured she best get on with that herself, now that she and Jonas had returned to the cabin. She removed her hat and pushed at the roll of her hair although she felt it was in place. "I'd, um, better change and get lunch on the table."

"Change of clothes would be in order," he said. "Something less fancy and some good walking shoes. I'd like to show you something. We can take a picnic lunch."

Molly liked that idea. She never felt ill at ease around Jonas, but for some strange reason, the thought of just the two of them in the cabin alone, having lunch, made her feel a little awkward. "There's bread left from yesterday. And ham left over from breakfast. I put that in a jar and took it to the creek."

He smiled. "There's cheese out there, too. Any pickled cucumbers left?"

"Yes, a couple of jars. Oh, there's a jar of tea out there, too."

"Perfect," he said, turning to leave the kitchen.

"Oh." Her word stopped him. "I can take honey to put on the bread for dessert."

He lifted a hand. "Double perfect."

Molly didn't know what was wrong with her. She felt like she'd just been asked out on a date. That stopped her progress toward the bedroom. She felt rather like she had when Percy took her to a fancy restaurant, to the fair, or on a Sunday ride in the park when he was courting her.

A sadness washed over her. She was feeling more excited about this mystery outing with Jonas than she had with Percy. Oh, she was probably wrong about that. Her feelings were tied up with the difficulty of her marriage that colored her view of what the courting had been like. She'd been young, naïve, flattered by an older man's attention, pleasing her aunt and uncle, being in love with the idea of being loved, and wanting a family of her own.

But there was no reason to compare Percy

and Jonas. They were worlds apart and entirely different.

And she wasn't being courted!

When Jonas and Sarah had gone up on that craggy peak, she sat in front of him on the horse with his arms around her. He could not do that with Molly. It would be too intimate. He took the wagon.

As if knowing of his reminiscence, Molly broke his train of thought. "What was your courtship with Sarah like, Jonas?"

Jonas appreciated Molly's making him talk about Sarah. Others seemed to think the subject shouldn't be mentioned.

"At the funerals, after the mine accident that killed her . . . and your . . . pa along with mine, I noticed her. She was the prettiest girl I'd ever seen. I wanted to wipe her tears away. But my grandparents were doing that. She was a student at Poplar Grove, where my grandmother taught."

Jonas had already dissociated himself from the mining community. His grandpa had seen to it that he got his education in town instead of in the mining camp. "My grandfather sent me off to a college in Virginia. When I'd come home from college, I'd see Sarah working for my grandparents, helping with chores and the cooking. In return they let her have their spare bedroom and provided her needs. Grandpa was a farmer and I'd help him in the fields. Sarah ate meals with us as if she were their daughter. I still thought she was the prettiest thing I'd ever seen, but she was only a high school student, while I was a big-city college fellow."

Molly laughed with him, knowing he was making fun of himself for being prideful.

"But none of the college girls impressed me like Sarah. She was smart. That's why my grandparents wanted her to live with them, to give her a chance. After your papa died, she had the opportunity to live with your aunt and uncle, but she refused."

"I didn't know that," Molly said, surprised.

He nodded. "She didn't want to tell you that. She thought you would think she didn't want to be with you. But she'd come to believe city life was best for you because that's what she'd been told when you were eight and she was thirteen. And, too," he added, "she had been taking care of her pa for three years when he died. She considered herself a grown woman."

He glanced at Molly who shook her head and sighed.

"You see, up here in these mountains, some girls marry at fourteen. They grow up quickly. But I don't want that for my children. I want them to know something of the world before they settle down."

He smiled, returning his thoughts to Sarah. "My grandparents treated her like a daughter."

"But you didn't think of her as a sister."

"Oh, no," he said. The memory felt good. "There I was, a college graduate with offers to teach in Virginia and at a school in the city. But once I laid eyes on the grown-up Sarah, with her hair looking like corn silk in the sunshine and those big blue eyes . . ." He stopped and smiled. "Like yours and Caleb's. All of you have the same eyes."

Molly smiled and shielded hers by looking down at her hands.

"She had a lot of young men wanting to call on her, but she said she'd never marry a miner and she didn't fancy the young men in school." Jonas smiled. "When she said that, she looked straight into my eyes, and I about swallowed my tongue." He chuckled. "Then she looked down at her hands like you just did."

He replaced his smile with a scowl. He had to stop comparing her with Sarah. When they'd played "Poor Tom," she had invoked his laughter before time for him to pat her head. But he'd intended to fake the laugh if necessary. He'd figured her hair would be soft like Sarah's. It wouldn't be fitting to touch it, even under the guise of a game.

Jonas had been impulsive when he thought of taking Molly up the mountain. This was part of his life, and he wanted to share it with someone. Of course he would share it with his children when they were older. But that was a long time off.

He'd begun to realize life is short and unpredictable. He needed to learn to live life to the fullest, stop concentrating on his losses, and count his blessings.

Jonas continued to coax Mac up and around a forested mountain until he turned onto a narrow dirt road that ran alongside a wide creek until they rode out of the trees and into a hollow so typical of the eastern Kentucky mountains.

Molly jumped down from the wagon before he could walk around to hold up his hand to her. She ran to the ridge from which one could view mountain peaks and hollows below.

"Way down there to your left," he said, walking up, "is Pine Hollow. That long building that looks about the size of Caleb's train car is the school. A little farther, which you can't really see from here, are our cabin and fields."

Molly's shoulders rose with her intake of breath. She put her hand on her chest. "Jonas, this is breathtaking."

He laughed. "Could be the thin air, too."

She boxed him lightly on the arm and turned toward the wide clearing of about ten acres. He gestured toward the wide expanse. "This is where the Fourth of July Festival will be held."

She looked askance at him. "Suppose it rains."

He jested. "Wouldn't dare."

"Oh, Jonas." She shook her head. "I think you just invited God to send a thunderstorm."

He laughed. "If so, we'll postpone until the next day. Come on. I want to show you something."

They walked into the forest where Mac was tied at the edge. She followed as Jonas led her up a winding trail until they reached a clearing where they could look down upon the valley where the festival would take place.

They came upon a one-room hunting shelter. The fireplace hadn't been cleaned out. Bedding lay in a corner. An old coat hung on one of the hooks on the plank walls.

"I hear the creek," Molly said.

Jonas nodded. "There's a natural spring here that runs into the creek. This was my great-grandpa's hunting lodge."

Molly looked at him quickly. "So . . . this is all your family's."

Jonas nodded and sighed. "All two hundred fifty thousand acres of it. There was a lot of unclaimed land in these mountains after the Revolutionary War, and the government thought that was good payment for those serving their country. It's been in the family since then."

She followed along as he walked outside. "There wasn't anything could be done with it for a long time. Some of it's been sold off for lumber, but getting the logs down the mountain on the river wasn't too practical. Now that the trains have been coming into Coalville and tracks being laid further up, I've had offers from lumber companies to buy some of the acreage."

"You would sell it?" Molly asked.

"Maybe." He looked at the shelter, seeing more than that. "Sarah and I talked about building our house here for the big family we were going to have. She came up with the idea. She was innovative." He looked at Molly and smiled. "Like you."

Molly turned away from the shelter and

looked beyond where blue ridged mountains spread out. Jonas thought her innovative? She thought herself a perfect dodo, unable to do a lot of the things these mountain people could do in being so self-sufficient. The only innovative idea she knew of might be her plans for the Bible school. And that was not an original idea. But if he didn't know, she wouldn't tell.

"I've already sold some of the land," he said. "They're our neighbors."

Our?

Of course, he meant his and Sarah's, or his and the children's. Or both.

"Down there, where we will have the festival, is land I thought about donating for a church. I can visualize a community growing up there. More people living here in the mountains instead of having to go to the city for jobs. Now that the trains are coming this way, we can bring the needed conveniences and progress to this area and still enjoy the beauty of the land."

Jonas would donate those acres of land? Daily, Molly understood more and more why Sarah had labeled him "remarkable."

Walking back down the trail behind Jonas, Molly thought he and Dawn were accepting Sarah's death more easily than when she first arrived at Pine Hollow.

"It's amazing how much Dawn can do with one hand," Molly said. "Having Nettie with her these past weeks has meant a lot. Keeping busy helps. I've not even had time to think of Dawn's resentment of me. Maybe she's beginning to see I'm not some kind of threat. If that were so, I would even . . . consider staying longer."

Jonas stopped and looked at her. He didn't mean to stare, but their eyes seemed to lock. Finally, he continued down the trail.

"I mean," she said, "if you want me to. Even after Dawn's arm heals, there is a lot of work to do. As busy as I've been already, I'm sure it can hardly compare with harvesting corn."

She would stay longer?

"You're so right," he said, trying not to show his pleasure. Molly had made such a difference in their lives, even if Dawn didn't know how to appreciate it. "You think you've had fun already. A combined corn-shucking is almost as much fun as the Fourth of July Festival."

Fun? Yes, the women had fun. Like the men had fun helping build a cabin, clear land, or raise a barn. But it was work.

As soon as they came to the clearing, Molly said she would get the picnic basket.

He walked past the wagon and to the lookout, unsure how to feel.

Gazing out at the valleys and mountains, Jonas realized that Molly was learning new things. Recapturing her childhood in a way. Feeling close to Sarah by doing what Sarah would be doing. Even going beyond with her teaching.

But this was temporary. A challenge. Something to take back to the city as a quaint experience. If she'd never known an easier way of life, it might be different. Most of the mountain people were unacquainted with city life, so they weren't accustomed to the modern conveniences like gaslights, automobiles, telephones, running water, and bathrooms inside the house.

Yes, in teaching history, he'd thought how interesting it might be to go back in time, to live in the Middle Ages, to be among the first settlers in America, to go to Europe and see the great cathedrals, to visit the Holy Land and walk where Jesus walked.

That didn't mean he would want to live in those places permanently.

Molly's enjoying learning to work with her hands, preparing for winter months when they might be snowed in or there were no goods able to get up the mountain to purchase, didn't mean she'd want to live here permanently. Just a little longer.

The circuit-riding preacher and the missionaries came to do their service for the Lord, but then they went back to the city for their everyday living.

No, a city person caring about the mountain people, getting involved in their lives, helping out, didn't mean they wanted to live that way.

When she called his name, Jonas turned and walked toward her and the picnic set out on the ground.

Molly had never thought herself a shy person and could hardly understand this awkward feeling that swept over her when she'd watched Jonas looking out over the mountains and then turn toward her.

Maybe it was their being alone like this that did it. She saw him, not as Sarah's husband, not as Dawn and Caleb's papa, but as a man she was getting to know — and like. He sat on the ground across from her. The gold in his brown hair seemed lighter each day, being bleached by the sun. His eyes were soft brown with flecks of gold in the sun.

He reached for a ham biscuit. "You're very unselfish to give up the conveniences in the city to come here, Molly. I admire you for that."

She shook her head. "I'm afraid I don't deserve your admiration, Jonas. I do want to help out. But my main reason for coming was selfish. I wanted to recapture some of my childhood. I wanted to find out what it's like to have a life like Sarah had. She was happy, Jonas."

He nodded. "Yes, I think most of the time she was."

Molly nodded. "That's because she loved you. And she had children. Those are things I've longed for and never had. Wasn't . . . allowed to have."

"You can't bear children?"

"Oh, I think I can. But . . . Percy didn't want them. He really didn't want me, Jonas, except to show off in public. He liked me well enough, but after our marriage I realized he married me because I was . . . young. Or maybe because my uncle had a business and a fine house."

"Well, I can certainly understand why he would be taken with you, Molly."

She saw his face redden, and he tried to redeem himself. "I — I mean . . . well, I didn't mean to imply anything improper."

Molly couldn't help laughing. "Well, he didn't marry me because I could use a cookstove or wring a chicken's neck."

Realizing the implication of that, she tried to explain. "He liked to show me off, but he was jealous, too, and the jealousy took over more and more. He presented me as if delighted, but if another man seemed to think so, or showed me special attention, he would blame me for that when we got home."

Molly almost stopped the conversation there, but realized talking about their grief and problems is what she had wanted Jonas and Dawn to do. She should follow her own advice. Her aunt and uncle knew much of the story, but she'd never talked to anyone about it like this.

"It gets worse, Jonas. Percy was embezzling from my uncle — quite a bit. The house you saw in the city when you came and asked me to come here was not mine and Percy's. We lived with my aunt and uncle. All of us believed him when he said he was looking for a place to buy or build."

She saw that Jonas was chewing his ham and biscuit quite slowly, as if unaware it was in his mouth. "You'd better swallow before I tell the rest."

Jonas chewed, swallowed, and took a gulp of tea.

"My uncle discovered that Percy was

wanted in Boston for having embezzled from a wealthy widow. He could be quite a . . . charmer."

She took a sip of tea before going on. "You don't know how he died, do you?"

"No. The telegram from you said he met with an untimely death."

"He was about to be arrested, Jonas. Public appearance meant everything to him. So much that he lied, cheated, and embezzled. He couldn't have faced arrest and imprisonment. The rumor was that on that cold winter night in February he was on some kind of errand in my uncle's automobile but got stalled on the icy bridge. Somehow, he'd walked to the edge to look at the river while waiting for help and lost his balance. Perhaps a sharp gale pushed him from the bridge into the icy river."

Jonas reached over and gently brushed away her tear with his thumb. "Molly. I'm sorry you had to go through that. I don't think Sarah knew you were unhappy."

She sniffed and blinked the moisture from her eyes. "Realization came slowly, Jonas. I was young and naïve and didn't want to believe my marriage was a failure. Through the years I had to accept not having things the way I wanted them." She shook her head. "Looking back, I know Percy and I were not in love with each other."

Jonas wished he could say or do something to console her. Maybe all he could do is what she'd done for him. Just listen and encourage her to talk. He remained silent while she took a few deep breaths, then lifted her chin.

A small light came into her eyes again. Her voice was soft. "Being here takes me back to my childhood when I had the feeling of love and family. All during the years I was in the city, I longed for what I'd lost. I didn't know that when I lived here I was poor."

"Poverty is not just a lack of money," he said. "It's not having to work hard. Poverty is when you have no one to love."

He suddenly realized he hadn't felt that poverty of heart in the past weeks. His family worked together, played together, enjoyed other families together like when Sarah was alive. He'd felt the joy of activity again, of being alive for the first time since Sarah died. Whatever he thought had died inside him had not died, but was simply buried alive. Like a seed that has dried out is hard and withered.

It would spring to life again in another season, if given nourishment.

Molly was good to have around.

She said if Dawn could accept her, she might stay through the harvest.

Stay? Birdie Evers had been a city girl. She said her love for Ira turned her into a mountain woman.

Molly loved Caleb and Dawn enough.

Caleb returned that love. If only Dawn could accept her, then . . .

Molly had made a difference in his own life. He reached for a piece of cheese. Her sharing today, letting him know what lay deep in her heart made a difference, pleased him.

But, he reminded himself, she wasn't here for his pleasure.

She was here for the children.

FIFTEEN

Molly couldn't be happier that Dawn was focusing on the work — or fun — of picking, cooking, and canning along with her friend and the women. If Dawn could get used to being civil to her when others were around, maybe she could begin to do so in private. Last week when Jonas again drove them to Coalville School, Nettie went along. The two girls practiced their verses in the back of the wagon, while Caleb worked at keeping his favorite chick from getting away. The chick now had the beginning of tiny wing feathers among its soft fuzz.

The women and children met at Beth-Ann's house today, canning tomatoes and talking about what each was taking to the festival.

"I was looking in my mother's Bible and found this recipe for mulberry pie," Molly told them. "I might try my hand at that."

They looked skeptical. She backed down.

"Well, I know I'm a rotten cook. . . ."

BethAnn and Earlene shook their heads and laughed. Birdie patted Molly's arm. "It's not that. It's just that Mother Jane has won the pie contest for as long as there's been a pie contest." She shook her head. "If you come up with something to beat Mother Jane, you'll be queen of these hollows."

Molly took in a deep breath and looked toward heaven. "I'm already halfway there." They laughed as she added, "I've been pretty good at being hollow at times."

Nettie wasn't there today, and Dawn spent much of her time outside with Rhoda and the little boys who had brought their wooden guns and rubber balls to play with. The girls were now throwing the balls over BethAnn's chicken house, and the boys were trying to catch them. So far, they'd been unable to but loved running to get the balls.

While the jars of tomatoes were cooling and they put out the fire under the pot, Dawn came up. "I want to go see Mama."

Molly's breath caught in her throat. "What — what do you mean?"

Dawn got that expression of tightened lips and nostrils as if Molly knew nothing at all. The little girl's shoulders rose with her intake of a deep breath and her gaze moved away from the women.

BethAnn explained. "Her mama's buried out back."

"Oh. Then, of course, it's fine that you go."

Dawn sprinted away.

"You think she'll be all right?" Molly asked.

"Oh, yes. The graveyard's just beyond Birdie's house and the school." She pointed to the school on the other side of the creek.

Molly watched as Dawn ran across the backyard, across the footbridge over the creek, and through several trees. Then she spied some tombstones and a hill beyond. No, it wasn't far.

Molly put her share of the boxed tomatoes in the wagon, as did Birdie and Earlene. BethAnn took hers to the cellar. The women were laughing and talking as they packed a box for Rhoda, which was payment for watching the little ones.

Their laughter stopped when wailing and Rhoda's voice came from the kitchen. "Now, Caleb, I'm just going to wash this off and put some ointment on it and you'll be fine."

Molly and BethAnn hastened into the kitchen. His knee was scraped and bleeding, but the wound was superficial.

"My 'eg is broke wike Dawn's arm. It hurts," Caleb said dramatically.

"I'm sorry," Rhoda said as she cleaned his knee. "He was headed for the creek in a place where the water's high. I yelled. He looked back, laughing, and tripped over a limb and fell on a rock."

"I know how that is," Molly said. "I'm not blaming you." She turned to Caleb. "Rhoda's got you all fixed up, Caleb. You can walk, can't you?"

He shook his head.

"Okay, you wait here with Rhoda for a bit, and I'll go get Dawn."

"I can get her," Rhoda offered as Caleb nodded.

"I'd actually like to see the graveyard," Molly said. "If you can keep your eyes on Caleb a little longer."

Caleb smiled at Rhoda, and Molly promised to be back soon.

When Molly reached the wooded area, she saw that Dawn had picked some wildflowers. She dropped to her knees at a headstone and laid her handful of flowers in front of it.

"I told you before, Mama. I'm sorry. But that don't do no good. I still feel bad about it. I didn't do the right thing. I'm just a — a bad person. I just keep being bad. But I'm

187

so sorry. I know you can't love me anymore. But I love you, Mama. I miss you so much."

Molly put her hand to her mouth to stifle a cry when the little girl brought her fists down on the grave, then laid her forehead on them and sobbed.

Molly turned and leaned back against the tree, taking deep breaths. Her chest ached from the feeling, and she felt she couldn't get enough air.

"What are you doing here?"

Molly opened her eyes and saw Dawn through a blur of tears.

Molly reached out to her. "I —"

"Don't touch me," Dawn cried out. "You listened. This was my private time with my mama." Her breath was ragged. "I hate you. I hate you."

Molly couldn't speak. Finally, after Dawn was out of sight, she could whisper. "I know. I know how you feel."

But the horrible realization was, knowing didn't mean she could do a thing about it.

Seeing Molly hurry across the cornfield, now about two feet high, struck Jonas's heart with dread. What was wrong now? She wouldn't leave the children to come out there for small talk. He let go of the plow and strode toward her. "The children. Are they all right?"

"No. I mean yes. It depends, Jonas."

He squinted against the sun. "What is it?"

"Caleb skinned his knee. But it's fine."

He stared. "You came to tell me that?"

She shook her head. Tears formed in her eyes. "I was behind a tree near the graveyard and heard Dawn talking to her mama. She was apologizing for something she did, Jonas. I think she feels like she is responsible for Sarah's death."

Tears streaked Molly's face. She took a deep breath and blinked. Her eyelashes were wet. "She saw me, Jonas. That made her feel even worse. She said she hates me."

He shook his head and put his hands on her trembling shoulders. "She didn't mean it, Molly. She's just —"

"Jonas. She did mean it. She takes her frustration out on me. But she said she did something wrong."

Jonas thought back. "I remember after the doctor came and Sarah and the baby were dead, Dawn cried and said, 'I should have run faster.' I didn't know what to do. I think I just said it wasn't her fault."

He felt the sting of drying salty tears on his face. "I've never talked to her about it. I've been too busy blaming myself. She'd had two miscarriages before having Caleb.

She always had a hard time. But we both wanted a big family. I've been thinking of me and my feelings and expecting time to take care of Dawn's."

"I need to get back," Molly said. "I don't want anything else to happen that I'll need to be sorry about."

He caught hold of her arm in a comforting gesture. "I'm glad you overheard Dawn talking to her mama. I'll talk to her later tonight. Sometimes I think we don't realize how deeply children feel things."

"I do, Jonas. That's why I'd like to ask a favor."

He nodded, hoping he could grant it.

"Before you talk to Dawn, let me tell her about my childhood and when I felt much like she is feeling right now."

"She hasn't been ready to listen to you, Molly. Don't you think she will be even more resistant now?"

"I'm sure that's what she's feeling. But if you demand she be at the supper table, I can talk then. It's not the most pleasant dinner conversation. But I think I'd like you to hear it, too. I just hope it won't make everyone sadder."

She looked at him a long moment, then turned and hurried back across the fields.

He doubted anything could make them

any sadder. He'd hung on to his grief like it was a prized pig.

Dawn was hanging on to guilt.

Molly was always saying she knew and she understood.

He was beginning to believe she really did understand.

He knew how much Molly had counted on his taking her, Dawn, and Caleb to the mulberry tree so she could get fresh berries. As much as they all had looked forward to the festival, and Molly wanted to make a prize-winning pie, this problem with Dawn took precedence.

As he neared the cabin, he saw Dawn sitting on the hill. Her dress covered her legs that were drawn up and her arm hugged them. Her forehead lay on her knees.

Soon after he followed Molly into the cabin, Birdie came riding up.

"I see Caleb has recovered enough to be wreaking havoc in the chicken pen." Her face clouded. "But how is Dawn?"

"I haven't talked to her yet," Jonas said. They went inside. Birdie's gaze followed his as he glanced at Molly standing at the sink, looking down into it.

Birdie pointed at Jonas. "You two go up there and get those mulberries. I'll stay here with the children."

Molly and Jonas remained silent until Birdie said, "Shoo! Scat! Go!" She reared back with her hands on her hips. "While I'm here I'll whip up something to eat and take back some chicken for Ira. That man never gets enough. I might even make up another batch of peanut butter fudge."

Jonas figured Dawn might need a little time alone to ponder the situation. Birdie might even be able to help. He hadn't seen Molly this distressed, not even when she talked about her disastrous marriage.

On the way up the mountain, they rode in near silence. Jonas stopped the wagon near a tree and tied Mac to a limb. Molly grabbed a basket, hopped down from the wagon, and walked fast toward the mulberry tree. She picked one and tasted it. "They're ripe," she said, but her voice held none of its usual exuberance. Had she given up on Dawn?

Jonas picked a mulberry and ate it. "You're right. Sweet and juicy."

"My mama found this tree. Oh, it wasn't this big then." She glanced at Jonas. "Well, neither was I. That's when she began to teach us the mulberry song. We had such . . ." She sniffed. "Fun." She moved to the side of the tree to pick from a low limb.

"Molly? You're — you're crying."

She leaned back against the tree and

closed her eyes. "I'm sorry."

"I don't blame you. This situation with Dawn is exhausting. She seems unreachable."

"Oh, Jonas. It's not just Dawn. I'm being selfish, thinking of myself. Dawn's feeling guilty brings to the surface what I thought I had under control. But now, I'm feeling sorry for myself. My papa gave me away, my husband didn't love me, my sister's . . ." She choked on a sob. "D–dead. I can't comfort a little girl and . . . I'm feeling guilty about my own mother's — I'm sorry."

Jonas took the basket from her hand and set it on the ground. He propped his hand above her shoulder on the tree. "You don't need to be sorry, Molly. I have taken advantage of your kindness by asking you to come into this situation. You've given so generously. And what have we given you but problems? You've helped me by listening. Now . . ." He lifted her chin with his fingers.

She opened her wet eyes and gazed sorrowfully at him. His heart went out to her. "You need to talk about your feelings like the rest of us. Let me help."

"Jonas, I don't think anyone can. I'll get over this. This doesn't happen often. It's just . . . one of those times."

"Then tell me," he said.

She drew a deep breath and gazed beyond him. "I feel like I can't even help a little girl. I'm no good to anyone. Our house wasn't far from here before Papa moved to the mines. He couldn't stand the house anymore without Mama. He couldn't stand . . ." Her sob caught in her throat. "Me. He couldn't stand me anymore."

Jonas put his hands on her shoulders. "Molly, he thought he was doing what was best for you."

She shook her head. "It's my fault Mama died."

Jonas listened to the story that Sarah had never told him. They had a new calf. When Sarah thought Molly was asleep she got up and sneaked outside. Molly followed. When Sarah turned at the barn door to look back at the house, she saw Molly.

The two of them sneaked inside the barn. They were looking at the calf when they heard their mama and papa coming. They hurried up the ladder to the hayloft. After their parents left, the girls giggled together. The night had turned much darker. Sarah lit the lantern.

Molly began jumping around on the hay, playing and saying she didn't want to go to bed yet. Sarah pleaded with her. Molly swung around and knocked the lantern over. Oil spilled out. A fire started between the girls. Molly backed away into a corner, screaming.

Sarah couldn't get to her. Sarah started screaming for her parents. They came as Sarah tried to get down the ladder. Her papa told her to jump. She jumped into his arms. Her mama rushed up the ladder. In her haste, she lost her balance as she stepped into the loft. Her feet knocked the ladder down. She ran into the fire. "Catch her at the window!" she yelled.

Her papa went outside, and her mama threw her down into his arms. Her clothes were already on fire. Her papa caught Molly, but the barn was already caving in. He couldn't get to the loft. The barn burned to the ground, and soon Mama was no longer screaming.

Jonas felt it, the pain, the loss, the grief, the guilt she was feeling. He enfolded her in his arms. Her head lay against his chest. He cried with her. He felt the rocking of her shoulders and heard her sobs. He soothed, "Cry it out, Molly. I think we both need to. For you, me, Sarah, Dawn, everything and everyone."

She nodded against his chest. He gently caressed her back.

After a while, he felt her body relax. His hands moved down her arms. She looked up at him. His hands came up and cupped her face. His head lowered, and his mouth touched her parted lips. They were stained with mulberry juice and tasted sweet. His eyes closed and his fingers were entwined in her soft, silky hair and his lips moved.

He breathed in her own breath then stepped away. He gazed past her but saw nothing — nothing but a man who had — what? Just betrayed his wife? Betrayed himself? Dishonored his sister-in-law? Sinned against God?

He then stared at Molly who stared back at him with wide blue eyes, bright as the summer sky. "Jonas," she said so low he had to listen closely to hear, "thank you for . . . comforting me."

She turned then, smoothed her hair back, and began searching for more mulberries.

Yes, he needn't kick himself mentally. Maybe physically but, like she said, he was comforting her. He had needed that sharing of grief as much as she.

Should he ask forgiveness for comforting someone? She had given his children her unconditional love, and with it came a feeling of comfort Jonas couldn't yet define.

On the way back, the only reference either

made to the event was when he said, "Molly, you need to forgive yourself."

Sixteen

Birdie had supper on the table under the cloth when he and Molly returned from Coalville. Jonas gave her two chickens. "One for watching each child," he said.

She didn't refuse.

"Dawn stared at that old iron pot for a long time," Birdie told them. "Then she went up on the hill. When she came in, she said her arm was hurting. That had better be seen to, Jonas. You know how dangerous infection can be when there's been a broken bone."

He nodded, thanked her, and bade her good-bye.

Jonas found Dawn in her room. He asked about her arm and she said it hurt some. "Maybe you've been working too hard lately."

"Pa, I can use my left hand better now than I could before. Pretty soon I'll be able to work better than ever."

There it was again. That implication they didn't need Molly.

He gently touched her arm. "Would you like to tell me what happened today?"

"Didn't she tell you?"

He nodded. "Yes, and she said she didn't mean to overhear."

"She spied on me."

"Did she apologize?"

Dawn looked down and nodded.

"Then you should forgive her."

"I'll try." She took a deep breath. "I don't want any supper. My arm hurts."

"I'll give you some laudanum."

He didn't know if that was just an excuse to keep from talking with Molly. His daughter's needs had to come first, and if her arm still bothered her in the morning, he'd take her to the doctor.

Surely Dawn wouldn't use her arm as a ploy to keep Molly from going to the festival. But judging by her prior behavior, that was a real possibility.

He decided to forgo the nightly cup of coffee with Molly. She was preparing the pie for tomorrow's fair after he'd raved about the one she made for supper. He told her it didn't need a thing as far as he was concerned.

Birdie and Ira were on the front porch

with her plants when he arrived. "Which one goes to the fair?" he asked.

"One? Why, Jonas McLean, I'm taking three."

Pastor Evers snorted. "She wants to bring home all the ribbons."

She gave Ira that warning look of hers. "Ira, how many ribbons have you earned for your preaching?"

He grinned. "No ribbons, darlin'. Just stars and crowns."

She harrumphed. "If you don't wipe that smug look off your face, you're going to see a few stars, but they won't be the kind that come from the Lord."

"Whoowee. Jonas, we better get out of here," the pastor said with a chuckle.

"I just stopped by to say that Dawn said her arm is hurting. If it's not feeling better in the morning, I'll need to take her to the doctor. But I don't want Molly and Caleb missing the festival. You know how Molly's been planning."

Birdie set down the pot of red geraniums. "Don't you fret. If you don't stop by here, we'll go down and get her."

"Thanks. I appreciate that."

Jonas returned to the cabin. The moment he opened the back door and walked in, he closed his eyes briefly and inhaled. Molly had her hands in the dishpan. Her pie was in the oven, but the aroma permeated the kitchen. "That's the most heavenly aroma."

"Now what do you know about heaven, Jonas McLean?"

He leaned against the countertop. "Didn't I tell you? I went to visit the preacher and Birdie. Now what could be more heavenly?"

She laughed. "I have heard that God has a sense of humor."

He smiled. "Those two are a joy to be around. Couples couldn't tease each other like that if there wasn't a lot of love between them."

He moved away quickly. He realized he and Molly just teased each other, and had a few times. But that was different. They weren't married. Maybe he should clarify his statement. "Sarah and I kidded each other a lot."

Molly nodded. "She was free to laugh. I was never free to be myself until . . ." She stopped suddenly and dried her hands. "Oh, listen to us. Talking about laughter and humor but getting all serious."

What had she been about to say? She didn't feel free until what? Until her husband died? Until she came here?

A questioning look came into her eyes. He thought he might have been staring. Turning, he spied the pie container. "Any left?"

"Two pieces. But you need to save one for Dawn since she didn't have supper."

He took the cover off the pie. "You and I can share this one, although I did have two pieces for supper."

"I only want a bite," she said. "I have to watch my figure."

If Sarah had said that, he would have replied that he'd watch it for her. But he just smiled and set the pie on the table, then went for coffee cups.

Molly awoke before the rooster crowed the sun awake.

When Dawn came to breakfast, she had an expectant look and declared her arm didn't hurt.

Molly had been concerned. She didn't want the child to go to see a doctor instead of going to the Fourth of July Festival. From all she'd heard, the festival was the highlight of the year. Everyone got involved, wanting to show off their crafts or abilities and wanted to see and taste those of others.

And she wanted to see her friends in the dresses they'd made for themselves. On the way, Jonas stopped by the Evers' place to let them know Dawn was fine.

Molly held on to her pie for dear life. If

she could get even a third place ribbon for her pie, then the people in the cove would be accepting of her as one of them. She was not just a city girl who knew nothing.

Jonas looked over at her. "You're looking smug this morning."

She smiled. "I'm afraid to say anything. It might jinx this pie."

"These womenfolk know how to cook, Molly. I've tasted their victuals. There's stiff competition, but I was speaking the truth when I said it's the best I've ever tasted."

Spread across Jonas's land were all sorts of activities taking place. People were arriving in wagons, on horseback, and in carriages. Many tables were set up, and men were putting doors on sawhorses to be covered with tablecloths.

A pig was roasting over a pit. Boys were throwing balls, and others played tag. Two little girls were yelling at the ridge to hear their echoes come back at them.

A couple of young girls came up to Dawn. They began talking about her arm. Others gathered as if that were some kind of prize. Dawn went off with them.

The sky was clear, and a cool breeze blew. Women were taking their baskets of food and prize entries to the tables. BethAnn rushed up to Molly.

"Your dress is beautiful," Molly said. "The blue makes your eyes look even bluer."

BethAnn smiled. "Thank you. That's what Tom said. Come on, I'll show you where to put your food and pie. Back here are the tables for the judging."

Rhoda came up to take Caleb and William to join the younger children being cared for by several young girls.

The tables were laden with every imaginable food. With care, Molly placed her pie with the others.

"It looks wonderful," BethAnn said and set down her jar of sourwood honey. She tucked her arm inside Molly's and introduced her to those she didn't know, including a young man named Harley, who was a teacher in the city.

There were crafts, quilts, and games including sack races, pig chasing, turtle races, and turkey shoots.

At the time she heard banjo picking, Tom came up and held out his hands to BethAnn. Off they went, swinging around on the grass. Other couples joined in. Molly enjoyed watching.

Several other players joined in with harmonicas and guitars. An older woman joined them, using two spoons to make her own rhythmic kind of music.

Jonas approached her and bowed. "May I have this dance?"

Molly laughed. "Jonas, I learned the waltz and the reel in the city, but I don't know how to do this."

"You don't have to know. Just stomp."

Everybody else was stomping, even the little children, whether or not they had a partner. Before long she felt like an old-timer, stomping, jumping, and laughing.

Molly was more certain than ever she would like to stay here in the cove and enjoy life with these people.

When the rousing music ended, the crowd began to clap in unison. Molly didn't know what it meant. Jonas looked down at the ground like something was wrong. Tom came up to Jonas. "This is when you always honor us with a song, Jonas."

Jonas crammed his hands into his pockets. "Tom, I haven't sung since . . ."

Molly knew what that meant. He hadn't sung since Sarah died. She tugged on his sleeve and lifted her chin. "If I can dance, you can sing."

"I don't know if I can." He walked over where the musicians were and took the guitar one man held out to him.

Molly heard the tremble and weakness of his voice after he strummed a cord. He closed his eyes and began singing "My Old Kentucky Home." His voice became stronger, and the baritone sound echoed around the mountains.

After the song, she saw that people who were sitting, stood. He struck another cord and began to lead "The Star-Spangled Banner." Molly joined in. When it ended, there were applause, whistles, and men throwing their hats into the air.

Jonas walked down to her.

"That was wonderful," she said.

He smiled. "Thank you. You weren't bad yourself. I don't think anybody else has ever reached those high notes around here before."

Someone rang a bell, and quiet fell over the crowd.

A big man yelled, "Folks, it's time to judge the contest entries!"

Molly nudged Jonas. "I hope the judges don't taste the pickles first, then the pies."

He grinned. "If I can sing, you can certainly win a pie contest. I'll go get Caleb. We'll eat after this."

BethAnn came and stood beside her. There were different judges at various sections of the tables. The desserts were last. She had high hopes for at least third place. When the judges tasted hers, however, they seemed to have trouble keeping a straight face.

The awards were called, the names read, and women walked forward to get their ribbons. Mother Jane's sweet potato pie won. Molly's didn't even place.

She couldn't understand why the judges didn't seem to even like her pie. Had she been so nervous she left out something?

She couldn't put it on the serving tables if it was awful. After the others took their pies away, she asked BethAnn to taste it. Beth-Ann put a forkful in her mouth, turned and spit it out.

Molly said, "At least the judges didn't do that."

Molly tasted it. She spit it out, too. "Salt!"

BethAnn nodded. "You must have used salt instead of sugar."

They both stared at the pie. After a thoughtful moment, Molly picked up the fork. She took a bite from beneath the lattice crust. Then she took a bite of the crust and spit it out. "The salt isn't in the ingredients. It's on the crust."

"Could you have sprinkled salt on the crust instead of sugar?"

Molly took a deep breath. The recipe didn't call for sugar to be sprinkled on the crust. She took the same sugar from the container for the crust as for the inside of the pie. Accusations wouldn't help anything. She laid down the fork and picked up the pie. "That seems like the obvious thing. I'll just find my basket and put this in it so nobody else tastes it."

She looked out over the crowd until she saw Dawn. The little girl stared at her triumphantly. Molly couldn't keep the moisture from her eyes.

BethAnn's gaze followed Molly's. Dawn spoke to Nettie. They turned and went to a food table.

"Don't worry about not winning, Molly. It may be a good thing. The cove women have the impression you're about perfect."

Molly swiped at her wet cheeks. "Me? Perfect? I can't even get a little girl to like me."

"They don't know all that. They take pride in the fact you sing and play the piano like you're some angel or something. So they'll love it that you can't cook." She placed the pie in Molly's basket she found under the table.

Molly remembered hearing a sound during the night. She had peeked out from her bedroom door and saw Dawn in the kitchen. She figured the girl was hungry since she'd eaten no supper. Molly had left ham and biscuits on the table.

She wouldn't accuse Dawn, but salt didn't sprinkle itself on her pie.

BethAnn's words penetrated her senses. "Next year, you can win. It's really hard to compete with Mother Jane, anyway."

Molly nodded but felt defeated. Not about the pie, but because she'd failed to help the one she most wanted to help — a little girl who'd lost her mother.

How could she even begin to consider living in the hollow or in town at the settlement when she couldn't be a part of her own sister's family?

No, next year Molly wouldn't be there — maybe not even next week.

At lunchtime, Jonas noticed Dawn sitting with Nettie and another friend. Caleb ran over to sit beside Molly at the table with BethAnn. The preacher manned the beverage table. Jonas found a seat on a log beside Harley Sullivan, a younger man who stuck out like a sore thumb with his bright red curls. Harley had worked for Jonas a couple of summers to help pay his way to school in the city.

He'd come home to visit his parents. "Don't get up this way much anymore," Harley said. "I've traded the hard physical work up here for the hard mental work in the city. Can't say it's an improvement, though."

Jonas laughed. "I think it's called progress. Becoming somebody. Making money. Get you a city woman and settle down."

"Speaking of city women." Harley gazed at the table some distance away. "I hear Sarah's sister is living with you now."

"Yep. That puts me out in the lean-to where you stayed when you worked for me."

Harley nodded. "My mama told me about her. I've already spoken to her briefly, and she was interested in talking to my parents after I told her they knew her dad. Um, I heard she's a widow."

Jonas didn't quite understand his interest. On second thought, maybe he did.

"She's mighty pretty, Jonas. And if she's anything like Sarah, she's one fine woman."

A quick answer sprang to Jonas's lips. "Molly's not like Sarah. She's lived in the city for the past fifteen years or so. Has city ways."

Jonas saw Harley's face turn toward him and felt his stare. The younger man spoke slowly. "There are a lot of fine women in the city, Jonas."

Jonas didn't know why he'd spoken that way. "I didn't mean it the way it sounds.

She is a fine woman. But . . . not like Sarah."

They ate. Jonas hadn't seen the mulberry pie anywhere. They must have snapped it up quickly. He had a piece of Mother Jane's pie. "This is mighty fine pie, Harley. Want a bite?"

Harley forked a bite. After a long moment he spoke. "Jonas, I hope you won't be offended. But I was wondering. I'm going to be around awhile, helping the folks with some repairs and all. I wonder, would it be all right if I called —"

"Well, sure, Harley. You don't even have to ask."

Harley paled. "No, I don't mean on you. I mean . . ." He cleared his throat. "May I call on Miz Molly?"

Call on Molly?

Jonas's thoughts were jumbled. A part of him wanted to say that Molly wasn't there to be called on. She was there for him and the children, even if things didn't always work out too well. No, he couldn't call.

"Did you hear me, Jonas?"

Jonas finally swallowed his bite of sweet potato pie and felt it sticking in his throat. He cleared it. "Well, sure, Harley. She would probably like to talk with someone from the city. Of course, the final say-so is up to her."

He had no right to say if anybody called

211

or didn't call on Molly.

Not a bit.

None whatsoever.

Seventeen

"I guess everybody's tuckered out," Jonas said on the way home. "Quite a different brood than when we left home this morning."

"Caleb ran all day long." Molly brushed her hand lightly over his head that rested on her lap. He had looked as if he were about ready to fall over, so Molly said she would sit in back with him. Dawn sat up front.

Molly hated her suspicions about the pie. She didn't want to think Dawn would do such a thing — disliking Molly was one thing, but taking such action against her was entirely another.

"You're tired, too, aren't you, Dawn?" Jonas said.

She nodded.

"Molly, I guess they snapped up your pie in a hurry. I didn't even get a piece."

Molly took a deep breath, not sure what she should say. "I had to put it back into the basket. The topping was . . . too salty."

"Salty?"

Molly looked from his to Dawn's profiles. His lips pursed in a thoughtful gesture. Dawn looked stiffly straight ahead.

"I didn't see you use any salt for the pie."

Molly didn't say anything.

No one else spoke all the way home.

After arriving back at the cabin, Jonas carried Caleb inside. Dawn hurried and held the screen door open for him, then she went to her room.

Jonas returned to the kitchen to see Molly setting the basket on the table. He'd been in the kitchen last night when she took the pie from the oven. She'd set the pie on the sideboard, and this morning she'd taken it and put it in a pie dish and covered it with a lid.

He had picked up the basket this morning. Now, he saw traces of white granules on the table where the basket sat. He ran his finger across it and tasted.

Salt.

He got a fork, took a bite, then spit it out the back door.

Molly glanced at him and away, as if she didn't even need to taste it to know. He watched Molly take the empty dishes from the basket, then the pie.

"Wait," he said. "Let's put the pie here." He took it and placed it on the table and moved the basket away. "Dawn," he called.

Dawn came to the door.

Jonas gestured to the table. "Let's all sit down, have a piece of pie, and talk about the good times we had today."

Dawn looked at the pie and at him. "I'm not hungry."

"You always eat something before going to bed. Don't you want a few bites?"

"No, Pa. I'm tired."

He forked off a bite and put it into his mouth. He had to spit it out the door again.

"This is full of salt." He ran his fingers through the granules and held up his hand. "Wonder how this happened?"

Dawn looked scared. She shrugged.

"No idea?"

She shook her head.

"I wonder," Jonas said. "Caleb must have thought he was helping by spreading sugar on the pie but got the salt instead. I'll have to teach him a lesson. Take him out to the barn and use the strap."

Dawn began shaking her head. "Caleb wouldn't do that." She pointed at Molly. "Maybe she got the salt and sugar mixed up."

"No. Somebody had to get into the pantry and take out the salt. It's here on the table. If it wasn't you, it had to be Caleb and he will have to be punished."

Dawn began to gasp and talk between breaths. Molly knew how that felt. She'd cried enough times from so deep inside it hurt to even breathe.

"It — was–n't Caleb. I d–did it. Maybe — maybe she — wants to w–whip me."

"No, Dawn." Molly took a step toward Dawn, but the little girl wrenched away.

Dawn began to cry. "I hurt."

"Your arm?"

She shook her head. "I hurt all over."

Jonas stepped forward. "I can't let this pass, Dawn. You're hurting yourself, too, when you try to hurt Molly."

Dawn ran to her room with a cry.

Molly stepped in front of Jonas as he started forward, his face flushed. His hands came up and caught her shoulders to keep from careening forward.

Her pleading eyes held his. "Please, Jonas. Let her be alone for a while. You spoke the truth when you said she's hurting herself. You need to be calm when you talk to her about this."

His hands lay on her shoulders. He took a deep breath, nodded, and stepped back "We can't let her take action against you like this. Where will it stop?"

"Yesterday you agreed I could talk to her. Let me try to help her understand that I know how she feels."

The next morning, right after breakfast, Molly put on her black mourning dress. It was perfect for what she had to do. Jonas had gone into the fields. She told Dawn to keep Caleb in the house.

Dawn's eyes swept over Molly's stained mourning dress. "Are you . . . leaving us?"

Molly took a deep breath. "Not yet. I will be here until your arm heals. But right now, I have a job to do. You mind me, and I mean it. You keep Caleb next to you. He must not follow me."

Dawn nodded, her eyes fearful. Molly meant to put the fear in Dawn. Her attempts at being kind and patient had failed. She didn't know what else to try. Caleb was listening, his eyes as wide as Dawn's.

Molly marched out the back door, slammed it behind her, and went to the iron pot. She looked back and saw Dawn and Caleb staring out the window. Dawn's mouth flew open. She came to the door and cracked it enough to stick her head out. "Is that my punishment? You're going to take my mama's pot away?"

Molly put her hands on her hips and stomped her foot. "Dawn McLean. I could wash your mouth out with soap. I am not some kind of monster, and I'm tired of you making me out to be one. Now, get in that house."

The door slammed, and Dawn's face again appeared at the window.

Molly turned the pot onto its side and bent over to roll it with her hands. She'd surely pull the muscles in her back. How did Dawn get it across the yard, beyond the barn, through the pasture, and up the hill enough for it to roll back and break her arm?

Maybe determination was the answer. Knowing Dawn would be watching from the window was enough to increase Molly's determination accordingly.

She began alternating with her feet to roll the pot. Ah, the land was slanted enough that the pot rolled fairly easily, although it preferred a zigzag journey.

A few uphill spots in the pasture required her pushing with her hands. Getting through deep-set places, not to mention cow and horse droppings, required not only the hands but getting on all fours doing some fancy maneuvers and getting the hips into it.

She stopped several times to wipe the sweat from her brow. Maybe Dawn hadn't tried to do this all in one day — nor in the summertime. She should have brought some water to drink.

She took several deep breaths and stooped down to begin rolling the pot up the hill. She got it up to arm's length and began to move her feet upward on the hill far enough to bend her arms and push again. However, her toes slipped. She lay face-down on the hill, feeling every rock beneath her. She could imagine this being precisely how the pot had rolled back and broken Dawn's arm.

How was she going to get out of this?

She heard Jonas's voice. "What, may I ask, are you doing?"

"Taking a nap," she snapped. "Can't you tell?"

"She's crazy."

That was Dawn's voice.

"I told you to stay . . ." She couldn't go on speaking. She had to reserve any energy she had, if there was any left.

"I locked Caleb in the chicken pen. And I had to go get Pa," Dawn wailed. "I thought you would break both your arms."

Dawn cared? No, she probably only cared that if Molly broke her arms she would have to stay here longer.

"Looks to me like you're trying to break your neck or your back," Jonas said. Unsquinching her eyes, she saw his booted feet next to her face. His strong arms reached down, and the weight of the pot was removed from her hands and outstretched arms — from her entire body, in fact.

Jonas turned the pot so the rounded part was turned opposite the curve of the hill. He braced it with his booted foot against the level bottom of the pot. "Dawn, go take care of Caleb."

Molly managed to get to all fours, then looked over her shoulder to see Dawn running across the pasture, toward the house. Molly looked up at Jonas.

He shook his head. "Why didn't you ask for my help?"

"It didn't occur to me."

He chuckled.

Molly snickered.

He threw back his head and laughed, saying between breaths, "I've never seen anything look so funny. Not even the cat when it gets its back up."

Getting to her knees, although her dress seemed to make every effort to prevent it, she heaved a breath. "Why can't women wear pants for things like this?"

He laughed again. "Maybe because most women don't do things like this."

She managed to get to her feet, although shakily. "All right, mister. Let's see you roll the pot up the hill."

He shrugged. "No problem."

He bent, turned the pot, gave it a good arm's length roll, moved his feet and yelled, "Whoa!" As his foot slipped, he turned the pot to keep it from rolling down. Molly put her hands on her hips and laughed then, while he looked at her sheepishly.

"Maybe if the two of us do this."

They worked out a plan. He would push, she would turn the pot and hold it while he moved up a few feet and began the process again. His final push over the top left him lying prone right below the pot. Molly tugged and set the pot on its bottom. "Don't want to chance it rolling anywhere," she said.

Jonas crawled up on top and sat, dirty and disheveled, as Molly looked. She pushed her hair out of her face. Then the laughter came.

Jonas looked at her, and it rumbled from him. They both laughed. He rolled onto his back. Molly got down and did the same. The two of them lay there, laughing until they almost cried.

Finally, Molly sat up. "I'm rusty, scraped, dented, sore in spots, and numb in others."

Jonas sat up. His gaze swept over her dress. "I've never seen a mourning dress get so much wear."

"Yes, it has come in handy." She looked out to see what Dawn and Sarah had seen from this hilltop. Looking around, she gazed over Jonas's green fields, some with yellow squash visible, and beyond was corn with long leaves waving in the breeze. Beyond and above were the craggy peaks and forested mountains that belonged to Jonas.

"I can see why Dawn and Sarah wanted this as their special place," Molly said, all laughter gone from her.

"Thank you for attempting this."

Molly nodded. "I don't really deserve praise. I did it mainly out of frustration."

"Still," he said, "you're a remarkable woman for attempting it."

Remarkable? That's how Sarah had described Jonas. And she was right.

"Ah, well," Molly said, always having found it difficult to accept praise, "I figure, if you can't move a mountain, at least move a pot."

A smile spread across Jonas's face and into his eyes. "You're good for me." He stood, held out his hand, and helped her up. "Now, let's see if we can get down from here without rolling."

She felt confident. He didn't let go until they reached the bottom.

Since she was already filthy, Molly worked in the garden and cooked lunch in that black dress, which had become such an important item in her life. Good for dirty work. The house was extremely hot, not only from the temperature but the cookstove, so she spread out a tablecloth under a maple near the creek and they ate there.

Dawn was quieter than usual, not even offering a snide remark or rolling her eyes. Molly decided not to try with her anymore, just take care of her as best she could, which didn't include much other than washing her clothes and cooking her meals.

During lunch, Jonas said, "Um, Molly, when is wash day?"

She looked at him quickly, and her mouth dropped open. She closed it when she saw his grin and the twinkle in his eyes. "I made a new schedule. It's do what needs to be done, when you can, if you can." She glanced down at her dress. "What I have in mind is to kill two birds with one stone."

"No," Caleb said, wide-eyed. "Papa said don't kill birds."

She reached over and patted his little hand. "No, sweetie. I don't kill birds. That's just a saying. It means I'm going to do two things at one time." She huffed. "Like you're doing right now. One, you're stuffing too much peanut butter and bread into your mouth. Two, you're about to squeeze the life out of that worm on your plate."

He gave her a *Don't-you-know?* kind of look. "This is for the fish."

"Just make sure it doesn't end up down your throat." She laughed at the way he screwed up his face and emitted a peanut butter mumble of disgust.

"Anyway." Molly looked at Jonas again. "It's so hot today, I thought I'd borrow your bathtub."

He snorted. "I don't have a bathtub anymore."

"The spring," she said. "I can wash me and my dress at the same time."

"It's cold," he warned.

"The house is too hot."

"Fine. In case there are any bears or mountain lions around, I'll take Caleb and his worm up that way and go fishing."

"Oh, wonderful. You can protect us with the fishing pole."

He laughed with her, then turned to Dawn. "You want to go with us?"

She shrugged. "I don't know. When am I going to be punished?"

"Dawn," Molly said immediately, "I'm not going to punish you. I didn't come here for that. I came to love you. And I do."

Dawn leaned over on the tablecloth with her fists clenched. "I'm bad, bad, bad."

Molly looked into Jonas's troubled eyes.

Caleb moved over to Dawn and put his hand on her back. "You're not bad. I wuv you."

Dawn rose to her knees and hugged her little brother. He asked, "You feel better now?"

Dawn whispered, "Yes," and Caleb moved back to inspect the worm.

Jonas took a deep breath. "Dawn, we'll talk about it tonight."

She nodded. This time she didn't run up the hill, but back to the cabin.

EIGHTEEN

After supper, and once Caleb had been put to bed, Molly poured tea for her, Jonas, and Dawn to take out on the front porch. The air cooled quickly after the sun set. Jonas and Molly sat in rocking chairs. Dawn sat on the porch at the steps, leaning against the banister.

The hounds did their belly-plop next to the steps. Their big, soulful eyes reminded Molly of how she felt. What was going to happen?

Jonas took a gulp of his tea, then leaned forward and set the glass on the banister. "We could begin with an apology."

Dawn got that hardened look on her face that Molly had come to recognize as a defense against showing her emotions. She picked at a spot on the lap of her dress. "I'm sorry I put salt on your pie." She looked up at Molly with moist eyes. Her lips trembled. "I — really am."

Molly could tell by the sound of Dawn's voice and the tears forming in her eyes that she meant it. "I forgive you."

Dawn nodded. "And, thank you . . . for trying to roll the pot up the hill."

Molly realized Dawn was laughing, or trying not to, in spite of her tears.

At least, at last, Dawn was releasing some kind of emotion. "Well, I wasn't doing that with the right attitude. I was . . ." She started to say she was mad. But remembering Dawn's saying she was bad, Molly decided not to use those words. "I behaved badly, yelling at you like I did. Will you forgive me?"

Dawn nodded, blinking away the moisture in her eyes.

"I have bad attitudes sometimes, Dawn. Everybody does. But deep inside I wanted to get that pot on top of the hill for you, because that was special to you and your mama. I understand that. It's like the mulberry tree is special to me because of my mama. And I want you to know, I'm not trying to take your mama's place. I know that is impossible. Nobody can take another person's place. My aunt never took the place of my mama in my heart."

Dawn stared at her, something obviously on her mind. "But didn't you like the city better than the mountains?"

"Never," Molly said.

Dawn wasn't convinced. "But everybody talked about all the wonderful things you did in the city and the beautiful clothes you wore, like everything in the city is better."

"Things never replace people you love, Dawn. I wanted to be with my papa and my sister. I preferred that two-room box house to the big one in the city."

Dawn didn't seem able to fathom that. She looked at Jonas. "Did you know that, Papa?"

"Not exactly that way, no."

Dawn was trying to understand. "So you think your papa was wrong to send you to the city?"

Molly thought for a long moment. "I'm not sure, Dawn. Looking back on it, I understand why he did it. He thought it best. But I spent years feeling resentment toward my aunt and uncle. That was wrong. I thought my papa didn't love me because he sent me away. Now I believe he did it because he did love me."

"Then you know why I don't want to go and live in the city."

Jonas had promised to let Molly talk to Dawn, but that statement disturbed him.

He stopped rocking and his feet came down with a thud. "Dawn, what do you mean by that?"

Dawn was hesitant. She seemed afraid. "I heard you tell Birdie that you thought about sending me and Caleb to the city to live with Molly. And everybody always talked like the city was the best place to be. Papa . . ." She began to take quick breaths. "I don't want to go live in the city. I know it's good, but . . ."

Jonas was flabbergasted. Apparently Molly was, too.

Molly got out of the rocking chair. She sat on the porch in front of Dawn. "No. I would not let you and Caleb come to the city to live. Not as long as you have your papa. You thought that's why I came?"

Dawn nodded.

Jonas watched Molly lift his little girl's chin with her fingers, then smooth her hair. Dawn didn't cringe or run away. "Is that why you . . . ?" Molly cleared her throat.

"Treated you so bad. You can say it." Dawn nodded. "Yes. I didn't want anybody to think I liked you. If I didn't like you, then Papa wouldn't send me away with you."

"He's not going to send you away. I don't want you to go to the city with me."

Dawn looked at Molly through her tears.

"You don't like me now, do you?"

"I like you, Dawn," Molly said. "And I love you."

"I . . . like you, too."

Jonas felt his own tears wash his face when Molly reached for Dawn and his daughter cried in heartbreaking sobs. He looked at Molly with her sunny hair hanging far down her back, her arms around his little girl, her soothing words working wonders. He had held Molly not long ago, now she was holding his little girl. They all liked and needed each other.

When Dawn's sobs subsided, Molly moved back. "I'd like to ask you something. That day in the cemetery —"

Dawn looked across at her. "I really didn't like you listening."

Molly nodded. "I understand that, and I didn't mean to. But I think it would be good if you talked about why you feel you did something wrong. You were apologizing to your mama. Is that too private, or can you tell me why?"

Dawn remained quiet for a long time. Finally she said, "You already know that I'm bad."

Jonas noticed Molly didn't correct her on that but, wisely, just listened.

Finally, Dawn spoke.

Jonas listened as his daughter poured out her guilt and remorse. He could see it as Dawn described it. Her mama was having pains. Dawn held her hand for a long time. "Go get your pa," Sarah had said.

Dawn knew her mama couldn't look after Caleb when she was hurting. He was crawling all over the place. He would burn himself on the stove or crawl into the fireplace. Dawn took him with her, although it slowed her down.

Dawn's words and his own memory seemed to mingle. By the time Jonas got home, he could tell things weren't right. He'd been there for miscarriages and the births of Dawn and Caleb. The nearest doctor was in Poplar Grove. Sarah wouldn't let him go try to find a midwife. "It's different, Jonas," she said. "Stay with me." She began to talk about how good life had been with him.

He couldn't bear to think of the rest. His baby, his wife — gone and he felt the guilt. He'd known she had miscarriages and difficult pregnancies. Why hadn't he taken her to the city? He could have taken her to be with Molly until after having the baby. He could have taken her to Poplar Grove.

His vision blurred as he looked down at his nine-year-old daughter. She had felt the guilt all along, and he didn't even know it. He'd been too wrapped up in his own grief. Thank God for Molly.

Now Molly was telling Dawn about her own guilt of having disobeyed and gone to the barn late at night, which resulted in her mother losing her life in the fire.

"That's awful," Dawn whispered. She reached over and held Molly's hand.

"For a long time I thought my papa sent me away to punish me. I thought he blamed me for the fire. I was to blame, but I was a child and would never want to hurt my mama. I have felt so guilty for so long."

Jonas had the feeling Molly was still feeling guilty. He spoke up. "That's why we need to ask the Lord to forgive us when we do wrong, or think we're wrong."

Dawn sighed. "I have begged God and Mama to forgive me. Why don't I feel like He has?"

Children could ask very difficult questions. "Well, you also have to forgive yourself."

Molly looked at him quickly. "You said that before."

"It's true."

Her mouth opened, and her eyes questioned. But it was Dawn who spoke. "How do you forgive yourself?"

Jonas gazed at the night, wondering when the darkness had come and the moon had risen. Much of the tension in his household had been caused by a lack of communication. He didn't want that again. Dawn was nine years old — old enough to ask questions. She deserved good answers.

He would do his best.

"Dawn, you've heard about Jesus all your life. You know Bible verses that tell us about His being God's Son, dying for us, and being raised from the dead."

Dawn nodded like that was common knowledge.

"There comes the time in our lives where it has to go further than what we believe in our minds. We have to ask the Lord Jesus to come into our hearts. We have to admit we're sinful, or . . . bad. We ask the Lord to forgive us. That's called repentance."

She nodded again, like this was nothing new. He knew it wasn't. Pastor Evers proclaimed it from the pulpit almost every Sunday.

"It doesn't mean we'll always do everything right, but we will try to live the way Jesus wants us to. When we ask Him to forgive us, He does. So it's a sin not to forgive ourselves. That means we don't sit around feeling bad about ourselves, but we go forward and try to do better."

Dawn looked out into the darkness, and he wondered how much she understood of that. Pastor Evers could have done a much better job.

In a little while, Dawn stood. "I'm hungry. I didn't eat much supper."

Molly smiled at her. "There's food in the kitchen."

Dawn stood, then paused. "Aunt Molly," she said tentatively. "Could we . . . plant flowers in Mama's pot?" She grinned. "If your dress is not too torn up."

Jonas watched Molly's face almost glow with tenderness as she looked at Dawn. She took his daughter's hand. "Tomorrow we'll go to Birdie's and you can pick out the kind you want."

After Dawn went into the house, Molly sat in the rocking chair. She took a sip of tea and returned the glass to the banister beside his. "Jonas," she said, "I've never heard that about forgiving yourself."

"That's something I tend to forget, Molly. As I talked about it, I was saying it to myself."

"I wonder," she said distantly into the night, where the sound of crickets became predominant. Wind whispered gently in the trees. "I wonder if I've ever forgiven my papa for sending me away. Or my aunt and uncle for taking me to the city. Have I even forgiven myself for feeling like I caused my mama's death?"

He drew in a deep breath. "Or I. It seems this is a time for all of us to let go of what we couldn't control."

"I've never discussed these things with anyone before. I was like Dawn in a way, except not as vocal. Since I've been here, being an aunt who was resented, I understand my aunt and uncle better. I would never consider taking Dawn to the city to live. I missed my family so."

His heart went out to her. "Sarah told me she missed you terribly. When she questioned her papa, he made her feel she was being selfish to want you here, instead of where you would have advantages of education and progress and not have to work so hard. Often I thought she might have wanted to be the one who went to the city instead of you, or with you. Life is not always easy here."

"Oh, Jonas. She had more in her few short years with you than I ever had in the city."

He reached for his tea glass. Did she mean she didn't want to leave?

She spoke quickly then. "Oh, I don't mean that the advantages of the city aren't worth

235

it. They certainly are. Easy accessibility to religion, education, automobiles, gaslights, bathrooms, refrigeration, telephones . . ."

"We'll be getting those before long," he said. "Can't keep progress out. And they make life easier."

She agreed. "But I always wanted to come back here. Although I did want to help you out and I love your children, I had selfish motives, too."

He smiled, hoping to encourage her to continue with her honesty. This seemed a night for it.

"Jonas, I know I'm just their aunt. That's what Aunt Mae always was to me. I think it would have been different if I'd had the maturity to understand everything the way they and my papa did. But I was a child taken from everything I knew and everyone I loved. At the same time, I felt guilty because I didn't appreciate it more."

He set his glass back on the banister. "Maybe they didn't know how to help you, like you and I were at a loss for weeks."

She nodded. "Looking back, I think they might have tried. Just like I couldn't get through to Dawn until she was ready, maybe they couldn't get through to me. I shut them out."

"Then maybe it's time you forgive your

aunt for not being your mother. Forgive your papa for not knowing what was best. Forgive yourself for — everything." He paused. "And, forgive me for not always knowing what a wonderful woman you are."

He looked over. Her eyes were closed, but wetness was on her cheeks.

As if feeling his eyes on her, she faced him, opened her eyes, and smiled. He knew those were tears of joy.

His hand was on the arm of the rocker. She reached over and touched it. He clasped hers and held it for a long time.

He felt something stir deep within his heart.

"Did you feel that tremor?" he said. "I think a mountain moved tonight."

NINETEEN

"It's littler than the other one. It looks awful," Dawn wailed when Jonas took her to the doctor on Friday.

The doctor spoke kindly. "Now, Dawn. This is temporary. Your arm is weak because you haven't been using it. Take it easy for a while until the strength comes back, and soon it will be just like it used to be. You can even wear the sling if you think you've overworked it. But you have to start using it."

On the way back home, Jonas cautioned her. "I know you're in a hurry to use that arm, Dawn. But do as the doctor said. Sometimes we want the end results and hurt ourselves in the meantime."

He remembered his own advice about communicating and how effective that had been the night he and Molly had that talk with Dawn.

"It's like our sorrow over losing your

mama. We had broken hearts, broken spirits. We have to go through a time of grieving. And I guess in a way, we'll always feel that loss. But we have to start reaching out to other people and other things. With your arm, if you overdo, you may hurt it. I think it's the same with our hearts. It takes time to heal, but if we go slowly, make the effort, in time healing will come."

On Sunday those words, "Go slowly," came back to haunt him.

At church, Birdie made the announcement about the Bible school that would start on Monday morning. She had the workers stand. Among them were Molly, BethAnn, and Earlene dressed like they might be going to an Easter parade. A couple of other women stood with them.

And one man.

With her arms bent at the elbows, Birdie waved both hands and smiled broadly. "Harley Sullivan has volunteered to help with crafts, games, and teaching the boys." She crossed her arms against her chest and looked toward heaven. "What a blessing."

Blessing?

It then occurred to Jonas that he could have done that. He had more teaching experience than that young man who used to work for him.

That evening at twilight, Harley came calling.

On Molly.

"Let's walk down by the creek," she said.

They disappeared from Jonas's vision, from the kitchen window, after they walked into a clump of trees that shut out the evening light.

After dark, he was sitting alone at the kitchen table, staring into his cup of coffee when Molly came through the back door, all smiles.

"That was a short walk," he said.

"Yes, we both have to get up early in the morning." She didn't reach for the coffeepot, but walked through the kitchen to go to her room.

His coffee was cold. He stood. "Yes, I'd better bed down, too."

She stopped at the doorway. "Oh, Harley will pick me and the children up."

Jonas stared. "That's out of his way."

She smiled. "He doesn't mind."

"No, I'm — I'm sure he doesn't." Harley Sullivan certainly wasn't moving slowly.

On Friday afternoon, parents went for the final program to hear the children sing, recite, and show what they had learned during the week. Afterward, Pastor Evers had them all go down to the creek where he baptized several children.

Dawn was one of them.

Later, when they ate what the women had brought to the schoolyard, Dawn came up to him and Molly while they were filling their plates. Dawn's face was glowing and her eyes shining. She put her arms around his and Molly's waists. "I'm forgiven, Pa, Molly."

"Yes," he whispered, and the three of them hugged. After Dawn ran off to be with her friends, Molly looked at him and smiled.

"Thank you," he said. "If you hadn't come here and helped plan that Bible school, this may not have happened. At least, not at this time."

"Oh, Jonas, seeing all those children learning this week and some of them taking Jesus into their hearts and being baptized makes me feel so good — like the Lord can use us, even in our inadequacies."

"You're far from that," he said.

She turned and spooned green beans onto her plate.

That night it rained.

He, Molly, and the children gathered in the front room. Caleb had learned he could play with his toys all over the room, instead of having to be right at Molly's feet, on her lap, or holding on to her as if she might go away. Molly was teaching Dawn embroidery.

Molly looked at Jonas. "This is one of the crafts the children were learning at Bible school."

Jonas smiled. He tried to concentrate on reading a book, but his thoughts focused on the pleasure this family-type group gave him, instead of the sense of loss he'd felt for so long.

After a while, Dawn laid down her embroidery. "My arm is tired."

"Rest your arm," Molly said. "The embroidery should help make your wrist and fingers stronger. Next time, you'll be able to go longer."

"Aunt Molly," Dawn said softly, "now that I'm not being so bad, could you stay? I really like having you here."

Jonas held his breath, and Molly seemed to do the same. Her fingers stopped. Her mouth opened and no words came. Finally, they did. "Your pa can't live out the rest of his life in the lean-to, Dawn."

"If you children are having a snack before you go to bed, you'd better get it," Jonas told them.

Dawn walked over and whispered in his ear. "You could marry her, Pa."

Marry? He stared at Molly, wondering if

she heard. Her eyes were lowered to the embroidery, and her fingers were moving.

His mind shouted that he was already married — to Sarah.

No. Sarah was gone.

"Get your snack."

I can't.

Can I?

It was as if Molly answered for him. "Jonas," she said softly, "if it's all right, Harley would like to take me to dinner at the restaurant in Poplar Grove tomorrow night."

"That's up to you," he said.

She shook her head. "No. It's up to you."

He stood, tried to laugh lightly as he headed for the kitchen. Looking over his shoulder he tossed out the words, "I think I can handle the children for one evening."

The children were asleep, and Jonas sat in the front room again trying to concentrate on his reading when he heard voices at the door. When Molly opened it, Harley stuck his head in and spoke to Jonas, then left.

Bedtime had passed a long time ago. Jonas got up to leave. "Have a good time?"

Molly closed the door. "Yes and no."

"Is something wrong, Molly?"

"Yes, there is, Jonas. I'm — going to have

to leave."

All sorts of possibilities hounded his mind. She was going to marry Harley? She couldn't take this cove life any longer? She'd fulfilled her purpose and now it was time to move on?

He said the words he'd heard her say so many times. Her reasons really weren't his business. He couldn't ask why, so he said, "I understand."

"No, I don't think you do. Jonas, could we sit down?"

He really didn't want to. He wanted to escape to that lean-to. He didn't want to hear that she was in love with Harley Sullivan.

She sat on the sofa. He sat in a chair near her.

"Jonas, there was a letter waiting for me in town. My uncle has had a stroke."

"A stroke," was all Jonas could manage. That was not one of the possibilities in his head.

"Aunt Mae says she needs me."

We need you, too, he could have said. Dawn was just beginning to accept the loss of her mama. And he . . .

No, he couldn't mention what he needed. He wasn't even sure. He could only nod. He had to put away selfish thoughts. This was another tragedy in Molly's life.

"Jonas, I know there are needs here. But I've never let my aunt and uncle know that I appreciate what they have done for me. I need to thank them before I can move on with my life."

What kind of moving on did she mean? Having a life with Harley?

"I suppose you need to go right away."

She nodded. "Harley had planned to leave sometime this week. So he and I will leave together on Monday. That will give me tomorrow to help Dawn and Caleb understand."

The next day was difficult for Molly. Any decision about leaving or staying in Pine Hollow was no longer her decision to make. Dawn listened. "Can't your aunt take care of your uncle?"

"I suppose she could. But they took care of me since I was eight years old. I need to go and let them know that I appreciate that. I called Aunt Mae from Poplar Grove. The doctors say Uncle Bob may not live long."

Dawn was silent a long while. "I wish you could stay."

"So do I," Molly said.

Dawn's eyes brightened. "Will you come back after you tell your aunt and uncle you appreciate them?"

"I have to find out how ill he is, Dawn. My aunt says he is paralyzed on his left side. I can't say what will happen."

Telling Caleb wasn't easy. He clung to her and begged her not to go. She told him that her uncle was sick and she had to go and help take care of him for a while. Jonas did his part of helping the children understand she had to go.

She was hoping Jonas might talk with her later, ask her to come back. She had tried to make it clear she preferred the mountains to the city, was needed to teach if she wanted to, and loved mingling with the women of the hollow.

Would he hold her like he had beneath the mulberry tree and ask her to come back?

He didn't.

It was Dawn who said, "When your uncle gets well, you can come back."

While Jonas stood aside, Molly fell to her knees and drew Dawn and Caleb to her and hugged them. "Oh, I love you so."

Harley and his pa drove up early Monday morning. They helped Jonas put Molly's trunks in the wagon, next to Harley's bag.

The only person on the premises who looked happy was Harley. Dawn behaved bravely, but Jonas knew well that reserve of hers and the kind of emotions she tried to hide. He felt it himself. He kept telling himself to stop being selfish and think about that poor man in the city who had a stroke and needed Molly — like he had.

Like he did.

The children and Molly again said tearful good-byes, and Caleb again told her to make Uncle Bob well and come back.

"If I can't come soon, you can visit me in the city." She looked at Dawn. "I said *visit.*"

Dawn nodded. "I'd like that."

Jonas didn't know what to do. Harley watched with a grin on his face as if he knew something Jonas didn't. But Jonas figured he did know. This young man, who had been Jonas's hired hand for two summers, was now taking off with . . .

With what? The woman of his dreams? Leaving ol' Jonas there to fend for himself.

Well, he couldn't cling to Molly like Caleb had, and ask her to stay. He was a grown man. He held out his hand. Molly extended hers and he shook it and couldn't find any words to say, except, "I can't thank you enough, Molly, for all you've done for this family."

Her eyes looked wet. "We have moved a few mountains together, Jonas."

He squinted as if the sun bothered his eyes and nodded.

They let go.

He and the children watched the departing wagon wheels stir up dust. They still stared long after the dust had settled.

His gaze moved beyond to the mountains. Yes, they'd moved some. But sometimes you get over one and another crops up. "Well," he said, "I'd better get my things and move back into the house."

"Want me to help you?" Dawn asked.

"If you'd like. But, Dawn, I don't want you thinking you have to take over what your mama used to do."

"I know," she said. "But I'll do what I can."

"That's all anybody can do," he said.

A little later he stood in the bedroom. Sarah's and Molly's clothes were gone from the closet. They both had slept in that bed. He would turn the mattress.

When Caleb wanted to run around a bush and sing the mulberry song, could Jonas do it? How would it be to sit in church and not hear her voice? Would he stop singing again? He'd have to sit at the table alone and drink his coffee.

He'd have to rock on the porch with his glass alone. No, he couldn't do that.

He didn't even know how to make sweet tea.

TWENTY

"My, you look a lot different from when you came up last week to get the flowers for that iron pot." Birdie gave Jonas a long look.

"I'm sad," Caleb said. "Mowwy went away." He stuck out his lower lip.

"Her uncle's sick," Dawn added.

Birdie nodded. "Yes, I heard that. I'm so sorry, Jonas. Is she coming back when he's better?"

Jonas shrugged. "I don't know."

She gave him a long look. "You didn't ask?"

The only thing he could think of to say was, "She left with Harley."

Birdie reared back. "Ha. That whipper-snapper."

Caleb began to flap his arms and say, "Wippuhsnappuh, wippuhsnappuh, wippuhsnappuh."

"Jonas," she said, "I know that Molly was thinking of staying in the hollow. But she's not going to come back unless she knows you want her to."

He looked at his children, who were staring at him like he was a villain. They were all trying, but since Molly left, Caleb asked about her every day, always at bedtime. Dawn wanted to know when Jesus was going to help her feel better about Molly's being gone. His daughter was beginning to question her faith.

Faith.

Hadn't he already seen a lot of mountains move? He'd even said it. Shouldn't he have faith that Molly would come back to them? Didn't he at least have to take a step of faith?

Birdie pointed her finger at him when he again looked at her. She must have seen a difference. "Jonas McLean, I'll be at your cabin early in the morning — in time for you to catch that train to the city."

Have faith. Have faith. Have faith.

That's what the train wheels sang while chugging down the mountain.

When he arrived at Molly's house in a horse-drawn cab, he saw an automobile on the road by the sidewalk. Jonas stopped and stared as Molly came out of the house, so beautiful in her city clothes. She stepped down from the porch and opened a parasol that matched her dress.

He'd worn a suit for this — and a hat. He removed his hat.

Molly's gasp and open mouth as she hurried toward him was like a sweet welcome. She held out her gloved hands. "Jonas." Concern touched her eyes. "Are the children all right?"

"Yes, in the way you mean," he said. "But they miss you."

"I miss them, too."

"I should pay my respects to your aunt and uncle."

She glanced toward the automobile. "The doctor is with Uncle Bob now."

He told himself he mustn't stall. "Molly, if we got married, you and I . . ." He looked down and saw that his knuckles were white from grasping the rim of his hat so tightly. Looking up again, it seemed a light turned on inside her. "For the sake of the children. I know how you love them and . . ."

His voice trailed off. He followed her gaze and saw a horse-drawn carriage pull up. Harley alighted, rushed up, and slapped Jonas on the back, then shook his hand.

"Jonas. Good to see you." Then, looking like someone turned a light on inside his head, he glanced at Molly and back at Jonas. He smiled broadly. "Molly and I were going into town. She spends so much time helping out here, Aunt Mae insisted she take a breather since the doctor was coming. Join us?"

Jonas glanced at Molly, who didn't second Harley's proposal.

She wasn't commenting on Jonas's proposal — or saying anything to Harley that would indicate she would accept what Jonas had said.

He never should have come here.

He should have known Harley would be courting her. He'd come calling in the hollow. The comparison stuck out in Jonas's mind like a six-story hotel compared with a one-level flat-roofed building.

Jonas could only offer a secondhand husband who had two children and lived the kind of life that depended on hard work and the weather.

Harley offered comforts and conveniences of city life.

Jonas's fingers began traveling around the rim of his hat he held in front of him — a sad comparison to the top hat Harley held. "The pastor of the church I attended when I went to university here made me promise to drop in on him whenever I was here. I need to do that, then leave on the first train in the morning to get back to the children."

Molly wasn't saying that he should join them. Nor was she saying they could talk later. Her silence was his answer.

Here was Harley, a direct comparison between a gentleman and a farmer/mountain teacher. How could Jonas have even considered offering Molly his children in exchange for a life of excitement in the city? He was a foolish man.

"I . . . must go," Jonas said.

Molly looked as if she might cry and whispered, "Good-bye, Jonas. Tell the children hello for me."

Harley popped his hat onto his head. "I plan to visit my parents as soon as I get a break from school. I'm hoping to have an announcement to make." His eyebrows rose, along with the corners of his mouth, and he flicked the brim of his hat.

"Would you like for me to call a cab?" Molly asked.

"No, no." Jonas lifted his hand as he hurried down the path to the sidewalk. With such a desire to leave this place and his humiliation, he'd likely be able to reach the depot long before a runaway horse could.

He'd rather walk.

He felt like running — from his foolishness and humiliation.

He rented a room in a hotel near the

depot. Somehow in his fanciful thinking, he'd imagined she missed him and the children so much she would agree immediately. He would then take her to dinner at a fancy restaurant. They would return and he would take her in his arms, like at the mulberry tree, but this time —

No! Such thoughts must not linger. She belonged to Harley now. They would come to the mountains and announce their engagement. Harley's parents would be so pleased. The hollow people would be pleased. His children would be glad to see her. She would bring gifts.

Jonas didn't think he could stand it. The heaviness in his chest was not from almost running down the many blocks to town. He felt like running all the way back to the cove where he belonged.

As soon as he got into his hotel room, he washed his face in cold water, trying to take away the burning humiliation on his skin and the stinging dryness in his eyes.

The water ran over his hands. He could hear her and the children singing, "This is the way we wash our hands."

There would be no more of that.

He had allowed seeds of love to grow in his heart and mind. He knew he and Molly had grown closer, had learned to be friends, had related better and better the longer she stayed.

She made him laugh again, hope again.

Obviously, this was not God's will for his life, or hers.

He must accept that. *Dear God, I didn't expect to love again. It grew on me. But now I must wash my hands of the entire matter. She can never be mine.*

He stared as the water flowed over his hands, fell into the basin, and disappeared down the drain.

Just like his hopes.

In less than a second, Molly went from feeling like a bird soaring high in the air to one that was suddenly shot by a rifle and dropped to the ground.

"If we got married," was only the beginning of Jonas's sentence. "For the sake of the children," he'd added.

Never had she been so grateful for an interruption when Harley arrived. Sarah had told her once she wished that Molly could know what it's like to live with a good man like Jonas.

Although Molly had slept in the cabin and Jonas in the barn for a couple of months, she did learn something about what it would be like living with a good man like

Jonas. She could not bear to marry him and be like a servant in his cabin, loving him but not being loved.

When she returned from her outing with Harley, which had been filled with activity and excitement that kept her mind off herself for the most part, Aunt Mae said Uncle Bob wasn't improving, but they could keep him comfortable.

"I hope he can hear me, Aunt Mae," Molly said. "I never told him, because I didn't know how much I appreciate what the two of you did for me."

"You were the joy of his life, Molly. He didn't need to be told. Telling my parents they were appreciated never occurred to me either. Come, let's get some lemonade and sit on the front porch."

They went out on the porch. It reached across the entire front of the house and was bordered by a white banister. Molly realized she had spent many good times here. She'd held on to hurt and guilt for so long. But she really never doubted that her aunt and uncle loved her.

They sat on the brightly colored, flower-print cushions in the white rocking chairs. The hanging baskets of vines and pots of begonias reminded Molly of Birdie.

"Molly, Bob and I often wondered if we

did the right thing. We knew you were so sad, but I thought we could make up for it and you would adjust. Then time passed. It seemed wrong to send you back then, and take you out of school and piano lessons, the church, your friends. And I was selfish. I couldn't bear to lose you after having you come here."

"Being with Jonas and his children has taught me that, Aunt Mae. But when I came here, I felt like I was being punished. I was just a foolish child."

"No." Aunt Mae reached over and patted her arm. "You were just a hurting child. I knew that but didn't know what to do about it."

"Aunt Mae, I don't know if it was right for Papa to send me to you. But it happened. I want to thank you for taking me in."

Aunt Mae was shaking her head. "It wasn't 'taking you in,' Molly. It was giving you a home and loving you."

Molly nodded. "I know that now. I guess I'm a slow learner."

"It's not always easy knowing the exact thing to do, Molly. Just as you've told me about Dawn and that you weren't sure how to handle her."

Molly nodded. "I don't know what my life

would have been like if I had stayed in the cove with Papa and Sarah. Maybe I would have had a loving husband and children, like Sarah did."

Molly turned her face away from Aunt Mae. But when she soothed, "Oh, my dear, my dear," she exhaled heavily and turned again toward her aunt, knowing she could confide in her about anything. She was a very loving woman.

"But I wouldn't have had opportunities that you and Uncle Bob gave me. I wouldn't have had the love you and Uncle Bob gave me. Without Mama, Papa wasn't the same. And Sarah couldn't give a mother's love. You did."

"There are advantages and disadvantages all around, Molly. We make a lot of our own choices, but some things in life just come to us that are not our doing. Like me and Bob never having children. And why did we live instead of your mama? Those things are out of our hands."

Aunt Mae nodded. "We didn't take you back there for a long time, thinking that would cause more heartache. After a few years, when I took you to visit — when the train tracks were finally laid to the town near Pine Hollow, Sarah was eighteen and in love with that strapping, good-looking young man who was getting his education, and she planned to marry him after he graduated. We knew you had never let go of your dream of living in the mountains again, but we didn't think it right to have you live with the newlyweds. Were we wrong, Molly? Was I wrong?"

"Until recently, I would have said yes. But looking back on it now, I think you were probably right. About separating me and Sarah I'm not sure. But no, I don't think it would have been right for me to go back to the mountains as a young girl, after having lived in the city for years."

Molly marveled that she could sit and talk this way with Aunt Mae. A couple of months ago, she never would have believed it. "Thank you," she said. "Aunt Mae?"

"Yes."

"I love you."

"Oh, honey. I have hoped and prayed for the day when we could sit and talk like this. I never had a daughter, so I don't know how to compare. But I have always loved you with my whole heart."

Molly nodded. "I know."

They sat and rocked and drank their lemonade. It reminded Molly of the night she and Jonas sat with their tea on his porch. They'd held hands and she felt so close to him that night.

She had learned so much in those two months with him. The blessings were so numerous, she must not pine for what could not be — just count her blessings.

So much was finally right in her heart and mind. By having that difficult time with Dawn, she had learned how to love and forgive — most of all, forgive herself.

She had so many blessings, she must not complain to God — just thank Him.

TWENTY-ONE

Jonas had just entered the church when Harley came up behind him. "Let me shake your hand, Jonas."

Jonas turned to face the young man who looked like the sun itself was shining inside him. "Jonas, you've been an example of what a husband should be like, and I hope I can be that to the woman I will spend the rest of my life with."

Jonas shook his hand. Yes, he'd set the right example all right. He'd fallen in love with Molly, and so had Harley.

Jonas led his children to his usual seat near the front. Before the sermon, the preacher announced that he was happy to have Harley back visiting with them and that he had brought along his fiancée. The people could greet her after the service.

So Molly had come, too. She must be staying at the hotel or with Harley's parents. She'd probably come by with gifts for the children later on.

Dawn and Caleb both looked back but didn't make a fuss. Caleb only said, "Wippuhsnappuh," twice.

Maybe they had accepted that Molly was gone for good.

That's what he needed to do, too.

Telling himself to guard his emotions, after church he gathered his children and walked up the aisle. When he reached the yard he saw a puzzling sight. People were greeting Harley and a woman, obviously from the city by the way she was dressed.

That was not Molly. Harley's parents were nearby, receiving congratulations, too.

The young woman accepted hugs and kept on smiling. She and Harley often exchanged glances that appeared to be of more than friendship.

Jonas told himself not to believe what he was seeing. He walked up to them. Harley looked at the young woman. "Marylee, this is one of my best friends, Jonas McLean. Jonas, this is Marylee Walker, my fiancée. She just finished her last year at the university where we met."

Jonas shook her gloved hand and for some strange reason felt jubilant to meet her.

On the way home, he warned himself that his joy was unfounded. Just because Harley and Molly weren't engaged to each other didn't make his situation any different.

Did it?

One minute he wanted to go back to the city and talk to Molly. The next minute he was telling himself not to humiliate them both again.

After a couple of days, he took the children and rode up to see Pastor Evers. "I need some advice," he said.

"You two go out on the porch," Birdie said. "I just made some hot gingerbread. I'll take the children in the kitchen and give them some with milk. You want some?"

As good as that sounded, Jonas said maybe later, so Ira said no.

Jonas told him everything. From his initial resentment that he had to ask Molly for help. The change she'd made in him. Her own difficult growing-up years. The mountains they had overcome concerning her guilt, his grief, and Dawn's fears. "I tried to keep the faith, Pastor. But this situation seems to be a mountain I can't get over."

The front screen creaked, and Birdie came out. "Jonas McLean. You didn't say you told Molly you love her."

He should have known Birdie would be listening. "Not in so many words. But I . . . We . . ."

"Yes, I heard you say you kissed, and you held hands. Now, does that tell a person you love them?"

"I guess not necessarily."

"And I heard you spouting that verse about faith moves mountains like that's the only verse in the Bible. Don't you know any other verses?"

He didn't know what he did to deserve this kind of reprimand. "I've heard a few."

"Well, try this one. Comes straight out of Corinthians. The verse says you can have the gift of faith so you could speak to the mountain and make it move, but without love you'd be no good to anybody."

Jonas looked at the pastor who shook his head. "Now you know where I get the inspiration for many of my sermons. Birdie makes a good point, Jonas."

But Birdie wasn't finished preaching. "No woman is going to know you love her, no matter what you do, unless you tell her."

Pastor Evers spoke up then. "Birdie, that might be the way to a woman's heart, but we know the way to a man's is through his stomach. I'm ready for some of that gingerbread now."

She stared at him. He sighed and said, "I'll love you even more if you bring me some gingerbread. Please?"

Birdie looked triumphant. "See?"

Jonas "saw."

But he couldn't believe he could go up to Molly, say "I love you," and she'd just fall into his arms. She might not even be in love with him.

Suddenly, something occurred to him. Molly had said, looking back, she hadn't been in love with Percival Pierpont. Now how did she know that if she'd never been in love?

Was there a chance?

He wasn't sure he had faith that she loved him, but without finding out, at least letting her know, he was like what Birdie said, no good to anybody.

He needed to find a way to show Molly he loved her, not just stumble around on the words.

Harley was still in the hollow, so Jonas talked to him about his plan. Harley was eager to help. After Harley returned to the city, he sent word to Jonas that he found what Jonas wanted.

Jonas didn't tell the children where he was going, in case things didn't work out right. But Birdie was more than willing to keep them while he rode the train to the city and went to the place where Harley said the gift would be waiting.

Since the gift wouldn't fit in just any conveyance, Jonas hired a driver and wagon to take him to Molly's, then took it to her front door.

Molly came to the door and opened the screen. "Jonas? What —"

"Molly, you gave me a gift, remember? I want to give you a gift that means something. So, here's a mulberry tree for you."

He'd rendered her speechless, but he mustn't be. "When I came here before, I asked if you'd marry me for the children. I thought if you did, you might learn to love me. But, Molly, I want to marry you because I love you."

He couldn't tell if she was about to laugh or cry or both. He supposed it was silly of him. She looked at him, at the tree, and back at him. "A mulberry tree," she said.

"If you think you can ever love me, let me know. If you can't, I still want you to know that I'm grateful for what you brought into my life and the lives of my children. I would like for you to be as much a part of our lives as you might want. They are remembering you as the beautiful, wonderful woman that you are. They love you, Molly. So do I. This is a symbol of my love. Can you accept it?"

Molly was totally shocked. That was the funniest, sweetest, weirdest thing she'd ever seen.

The mulberry song had been Caleb's connection with his mother and with her. The mulberry pie incident is what brought her and Dawn together in honesty.

Now she must be honest with Jonas and herself. "Jonas, is this because you see some of Sarah in me?"

He took a deep breath. "I kept telling myself that. I felt unfaithful when I saw you instead of Sarah. I tried so hard. But, Molly, it is you. Yes, I see Sarah in you. But, I love Molly Pierpont — for herself."

Molly looked at him, the sincerity in his eyes, in his words — remembered his lips on hers when they both tasted of mulberries. Now, Jonas was using the mulberry tree as a symbol of his love and his hope that she could love him.

She reached out and grasped the trunk of the small tree, trying to find the words to respond. Upon hearing wailing from the parlor and her aunt calling her name, she had to say, "Jonas, my uncle died today."

■ ■ ■ ■

Jonas went inside and expressed his condolences to Aunt Mae and his obligation to return to his children. He bade them goodbye, saying, "God bless" to Aunt Mae and another sincere "thank you" to Molly.

"Thank you," she returned, while holding the hand of her aunt, who smiled despite her tears.

On the ride back up the mountain, he did not feel embarrassment or rejection. Even if she couldn't return his love the way he wanted, she knew she was loved. He felt good about that.

Leaving the flatlands and seeing mountain peaks coming into view, he thought how that train ride was like life. It's full of curves — up and down, around and around and sometimes you feel like you're going in circles and can't see the destination.

Even if he could not have Molly, he learned that he could love again. Molly couldn't replace Sarah, just as Dawn and Caleb couldn't replace the children he and Sarah had lost.

It wasn't about replacement.

It was just another step in life.

I've learned, Lord, he prayed to the rhythm

269

of the train puffing around the mountains, *that I can make it without my Sarah, without my babies, and now — even without Molly. Maybe You brought her into my life to thaw out my frozen heart, to teach my children what sacrificial love is, to have them realize they can be loved and can love again.*

I don't understand everything. In fact I don't understand much at all. But I understand my attitude makes all the difference. I can look outward and see evil or good, ugliness or beauty. I can look inside for that, too. Thank You, Lord, that You can take away the bitterness and replace it with sweet.

What lies beyond life is better — and eternal.

But while I'm here, Lord, I'm now trusting You with all my heart and mind and soul. Here's my life. When I take it back, forgive me.

Help me not to pout. Just trust You.

Someday I'll be up there with You and I hope to hear, "Well done, good and faithful servant."

And, Lord, I'm not asking You for Molly. Maybe that's not Your plan. If it's not, I'm not going to like it, but I'm going to trust You anyway. The best I can.

After he returned home, Dawn and Caleb seemed to accept his answer; he couldn't say when Molly would return for a visit, but he knew she would not abandon them altogether. They prayed for her each night.

He prayed silently that she would find the love she deserved.

TWENTY-TWO

"Look, Pa, look!"

Jonas stood from where he'd been bending over in the cabbage patch.

Caleb shouted, "Mama!" He looked at Jonas and stuck out his lip and changed it to, "Mowwy," for Molly.

Which is it? Jonas wondered.

The children ran toward the wagon where the driver was taking the mulberry tree out of the back. Molly knelt and they hugged, all talking at the same time.

When Jonas walked up, Molly stood and faced him. "The city's no place for a mulberry tree."

He dared to dream this beautiful creature, with her hair the color of corn silk shining in the afternoon sunlight and her eyes as blue as the sky, might be coming to him. Or, was she returning the tree?

"Are you returning the tree?"

"I'm returning me. Jonas McLean, you

asked me to marry you and don't you go backing out."

"Never," he said.

The driver called, "Sir, could you help me with the trunks?"

"Maybe you'd better get your wagon, Jonas. We can take them to Birdie's, and if it's not convenient for me to stay with them until the wedding, we can take them to town and I'll stay at the hotel."

Jonas glanced at the cabin. "I do have a place here."

"Why, Jonas McLean. Wash your mouth with soap. An aunt can stay in your house, but a fiancée cannot. I expect to be courted before the wedding."

"My pleasure, ma'am," he said and told the driver he'd be right there with his wagon.

After they put the trunks in Jonas's wagon, while the children were filling Molly in on what they'd been doing and all that was going on, Jonas went into the barn. He returned with a shovel.

"Maybe we'd better plant this near the creek," Molly said. "Mulberries drop to the ground easily and can be quite messy on shoes and bare feet. I don't want my house tracked up."

"Sassy as Birdie." He grinned, so full of

joy and excitement he could hardly contain it. From the looks of Molly, he thought she felt the same. "By the creek," he said. "That will do until we have to dig it up and plant it near our new house up the mountain."

Molly blinked at the moisture he saw in her loving eyes, and she nodded.

They went to the creek, Jonas dug a hole and planted the tree. He held out his hands. They danced around the tree and sang the mulberry song.

"I've never heard a more romantic song," Molly said and laughed.

Jonas gazed into her eyes. "Neither have I. And it's coming straight from my heart."

He thought he could stand it no longer. "Children, go get a couple of buckets so we can water the tree. Hurry."

They took off.

"I was so afraid you might not love me."

"Oh, I do, Jonas. When I knew I was falling in love with you, I tried to be cautious, not wanting my childhood dreams of returning home and having a family to be mistaken for love. I knew I loved you that day when we kissed and you tasted like mulberries."

"So did you. I almost died of the sweetness."

She smiled. "I would have come sooner, but I had to make sure Aunt Mae would be all right. Her sister, Edna, came, and they insisted I leave and come here, where Aunt Mae said I belonged."

Yes, this is where she belonged. He embraced her. Their lips met while they stood by the mulberry tree. This time he was in no hurry to move away.

When they broke the embrace, she lay her head against his chest. She whispered, "I feel like I've come home, Jonas. I'm home."

Since neither Jonas nor Molly wanted to waste any time before getting married, Aunt Mae and Edna came to help with plans. Jonas moved back into the lean-to and gave Mae and Edna the bedroom. Edna's husband had been dead for many years. Her children had married and moved away, and she missed her grandchildren.

The two women doted on Dawn and Caleb and found the mountain way of life quite challenging. Molly stayed with Birdie and Pastor Evers.

Jonas courted Molly. He took her for long walks along the creek, up the mountain to talk about the house they could plan for their present family and any children they might have later.

He took her to dinner at the hotel in Poplar Grove, and Molly proudly sported the ring the two of them picked out at a jewelry store when they'd gone down to bring Mae and Edna to the mountains.

"I've already had a big wedding," Molly said to Jonas one evening when he returned her to the Evers' home. "This time, I'm not planning a wedding. I'm planning a marriage."

"Don't you want the ceremony to be in the church?" Jonas asked.

Molly thought. "Pastor Evers says a church isn't a building, it's the people. So I'd like it to be outdoors on the land you're donating to the church. Where we had the festival."

"Suppose it rains?"

She said what he had said about the festival. "Then we'll have it the next day."

The following day they shared their plans with Mae and Edna.

Aunt Mae said, "Someday I hope I'll be more like a grandmother to the children than their great-aunt."

"Aunt Mae, I know the children will love you as much as I do."

"Thank you, dear." She placed her hand on her heart and looked like she might be having a nervous attack. Excitement shone in her eyes. "Well, considering their ages, I'm way past spoiling them. We'll just have to make up for that. So, while you and Jonas are on your honeymoon, the children can stay with me in the city. Edna and I can take care of them."

"I don't know what Jonas will say."

Aunt Mae straightened her shoulders. "I'm going to be a proper grandmother. I have something to say about this. Where are you going on your honeymoon and for how long? I need to start making plans."

Had Aunt Mae been that excited when she expected Molly to come and live with her and Uncle Bob? Oh, how Molly must have robbed her of that enthusiasm, much like Dawn had put a damper on Molly's excitement.

Aunt Mae looked at Dawn, then Caleb. "Just as soon as they say 'I do,' you can call me Grandmama."

"Gammama," Caleb said.

Mae hugged him. "Oh, you precious boy."

Dawn gave her a long look, then smiled. "I never had a grandmama before."

Molly went over and put her hand on Mae's shoulder. "I think it's time I called you Mama."

Tears sparkled in Mae's eyes. She put her hand on Molly's. "Oh, honey. You've made me the happiest woman in the world."

"I love you," Molly said, wishing the

whole world could hear her. "I really love you."

Molly sat in a carriage with Harley seated as the driver, surprised at the big crowd that had gathered for her wedding. Birdie must have invited those from Coalville, Poplar Grove, Pine Hollow, and the Black Mountains. There were at least a hundred people, if not more. They stood in rows, dressed in their finery, leaving a grassy aisle for Molly to walk down, toward the structure held up by a trellis Birdie had decorated with vines, pastel narcissus, and baby's breath.

Jonas and Pastor Evers took their places beneath the structure.

Birdie had put herself in charge of the music and there'd been no rehearsal, so Molly didn't know what to expect. She was pleased when two men who had played at the festival stood and played the hauntingly beautiful "Love Divine, All Loves Excelling" on harmonicas.

Aunt Mae cued Caleb to begin his trek down the aisle. He was the most adorable ring bearer ever in his dark suit with short pants, his blond hair gleaming in the sunshine and his eyes straight ahead. He walked slowly, holding the white cushion in front of him.

Dawn, looking beautiful in her new blue dress, scattered pink rose petals and took her place beside Caleb.

Molly exited the carriage. Aunt Edna straightened Molly's long veil and assured her that she looked beautiful. She had chosen an ivory gown with a high neck, long sleeves, and a bodice of seed pearls and lace. A blue sash adorned her waist. Aunt Edna handed her the bouquet of pink roses and baby's breath.

To Molly's delight, Marylee stood opposite Dawn and Caleb. She began to sing in a lovely soprano voice, "O Perfect Love."

Aunt Edna nodded, and Molly took a step. She almost laughed, realizing this was the spot where she hadn't won a prize for a pie. Now she walked on rose petals toward the most handsome man in the world, looking so grand in his dark blue suit, light blue shirt, with a white flower in his lapel.

He looked like she felt — about ready to burst with happiness. He held out his arm. She placed her hand on it and they faced Pastor Evers.

"Friends, we are gathered here today to join this man and this woman in holy matrimony. . . ."

After Pastor Evers said, "You may kiss the

bride," Jonas did. That initiated applause, shouts, harmonica playing, guitar picking, and men began singing, "Here We Go 'round the Mulberry Bush." Everyone laughed.

With her hands on her hips, Molly shook her finger at Jonas. "You did that!"

He grinned. "Well, it's our song."

"So it is," she said. And he kissed the bride again.

Caleb tugged on their clothes. Jonas picked him up. "Caleb, Molly's going to live with us now. It's all right now if you call her Mama."

Molly touched his arm. "But you don't have to. I am your Aunt Molly. Your mama is in heaven. She loved you very much."

He nodded and looked like he understood. After a thoughtful moment, his face broke into a smile. He boldly proclaimed, "Mama."

"Oh." That sweet embrace of his went straight to her heart. After a long moment, she opened her eyes. Dawn's gaze met hers. Molly let go of Caleb and stood.

Dawn took a step closer and smiled tentatively.

Molly reached for her hands and held them. "Dawn, you don't have to even try to call me Mama. Nobody can replace your mama. But I can try to do the things a mama does."

Dawn wrinkled her nose and got a mischievous look in her eyes. "Some not too well."

The playful duck of Dawn's head meant the world to Molly. "You're right. But we'll make do. And we will never forget your mama. My being your papa's wife doesn't mean that he loves your mama any less. You will understand this when you're older. You'll have a man in your life, and children, and you'll love them completely. You won't love your papa and Caleb any less. There's room in the heart for many loves, without having to let any of them go."

Dawn nodded. Molly knew the young girl was trying to understand. She knew, too, such a thing was not fully understandable until she experienced it. Molly hadn't really understood the wonder of being loved by a man until Jonas. Nor had she felt that indefinable, all-encompassing joy of love until Jonas.

Dawn sighed heavily. "This is what I'm going to do. I will call you the first part of your name. It's spelled different, but sounds like 'Ma.' Some of my friends call their mama's 'Ma.' How about that?"

That was a huge step for a girl like Dawn.

"That would be fine. And if you slip and call me 'Aunt Molly' that's fine, too. Just don't call me anything like . . ."

She couldn't think of what she didn't want to be called. Dawn said it. "Like . . . a scared cat."

"Ohhh," Molly quipped. "Now you're thinking cows and chickens."

Dawn laughed. "Exactly."

Molly's laughter joined her. What a beautiful sound. Then just as quickly, Dawn grew serious again, looking uncertain. "I might forget to stop at 'Ma' and say 'Mama.' "

Molly could only whisper, "That's fine."

Dawn came into her outstretched arms and held her tightly around the waist.

Enfolding her, Molly said, "I love you, Dawn. With all my heart."

She felt Dawn's nod and heard her whisper. "I love you — Ma." She was almost certain that was followed by another "ma." That didn't matter so much. What mattered was the feeling of love they both shared in that embrace. She felt Dawn's acceptance.

She looked over at Jonas and Caleb, who came to join in the embracing. With Jonas's hand on Dawn's shoulder and the other hand in Caleb's, his lips formed the words, "I love you."

■ ■ ■ ■

Aunt Mae came up and held out her hand to Caleb, who looked up at her with big blue eyes. Molly had a sneaky feeling Aunt Mae had won his heart.

Aunt Mae led him away to the food tables for the three-tiered cake Birdie had made. BethAnn and Earlene, looking like city women, served tea and lemonade.

Edna handed an envelope to Molly. She gasped. "Oh, Aunt Edna." She looked around. Jonas was holding out his plate for cake. "Jonas, come here."

"Can't you see I'm getting a piece of cake? Are you starting to nag already?" he said with a wink.

"Well, I guess I can go on my honeymoon alone."

"Whoa!" He set his plate down in a hurry and ran toward her, causing others to laugh. "No, you definitely will not," he said, putting his arm around her waist.

"Jonas," she warned.

"You're my wife," he said possessively.

She almost couldn't look away from his loving eyes. Yes, she was his wife. She leaned toward him. "Look at this."

The playfulness left his face as he seriously regarded the train tickets in his hand. Two round-trip tickets to Charleston.

"That's my home," Edna said. "I can't leave Mae to take care of those two rambunctious young'uns by herself. I'm going to stay with her awhile anyway. So you two just go to my house — it's at the beach — and make yourself at home."

Molly feared he wouldn't accept such a generous gift. He let go of her waist and held out his arms to Edna.

"Thank you — Aunt Edna."

They embraced, then she stepped back. "*Now,* he claims relation."

He spoke seriously. "I'd be honored to have you as an aunt."

"Well, you've got me, like it or not. And I guess one of these days I'll just have to share my house with my — with Mae's grandchildren. It's a great vacation spot."

Aunt Mae gave them a generous monetary gift.

Later, Jonas said, "I think I got the best of the deal here, Molly. I've married into a very fine, generous, loving family. You women are the best."

"I'm beginning to realize that, too, Jonas. A family shares what they have. Imagine if you had refused Edna's and Mae's gifts."

"It would have been wrong. And I could see Aunt Mae's need to shower love on my — our children. She wants to be a grandma."

His lips were very close to hers. She looked into his loving eyes. "For a while," she said, "I thought loving you was a mountain I couldn't move."

"Life is full of mountains, but we can move them." Right before his lips touched hers, he added, "with love."

MOLLY'S MULBERRY CRUMBLE

Filling

6 cups mulberries (any species)
1/2 cup orange juice
2 tablespoons arrowroot
1 1/2 tablespoons wild mint
2 teaspoons vanilla extract
1/2 teaspoon almond extract
2 tablespoons honey

Topping

2 1/2 cups fresh bread crumbs
1 cup corn oil
1 cup chopped nuts (any kind)
1/2 teaspoon salt
1 teaspoon ground cinnamon

Pour filling into baking dish or pan.
Press topping on top of filling, sprinkle the
cinnamon on top.
Bake at 350 degrees for about 40 minutes
until topping is golden brown.
Serves 6 — serve hot or cold

Do not sprinkle with salt.

ABOUT THE AUTHOR

Yvonne Lehman is an award-winning, best-selling author of 42 books, including mainstream, mystery, romance, young adult, and women's fiction. Recent books are *Carolina, South Carolina, Coffee Rings,* a novella in the collection *Schoolhouse Brides,* and *Moving the Mountain.* Founder and director of her own writers conference for 17 years, she now directs the Blue Ridge Mountains Christian Writers Conference held annually at the Ridgecrest/LifeWay Conference Center near Asheville, North Carolina.

The employees of Thorndike Press hope you have enjoyed this Large Print book. All our Thorndike, Wheeler, and Kennebec Large Print titles are designed for easy reading, and all our books are made to last. Other Thorndike Press Large Print books are available at your library, through selected bookstores, or directly from us.

For information about titles, please call:
   (800) 223-1244

or visit our Web site at:
   http://gale.cengage.com/thorndike

To share your comments, please write:
   Publisher
   Thorndike Press
   295 Kennedy Memorial Drive
   Waterville, ME 04901